Instincts long dead became alive again in Buck.

In vague ways he remembered back to the youth of his breed, to the time wild dogs ranged in packs and killed their meat as they ran it down. It was no task for him to learn to fight with cut and slash and the quick wolf snap. His forgotten ancestors had fought in this manner. They activated the old life instinctively within him, and the old tricks of his breed became his tricks. They came to him without effort or discovery, as though they had always been his. And when, on the still, cold nights, he pointed his nose at a star and howled long and wolflike, it was his ancestors, dead and dust, pointing nose at star and howling down through the centuries and through him.

JACK LONDON

The

CALL

of the

WILD

Edited by Barbara Solot

Afterword by Jonathan Kelley

TP **THE TOWNSEND LIBRARY**

THE CALL OF THE WILD

TP THE TOWNSEND LIBRARY

For more titles in the Townsend Library,
visit our website: **www.townsendpress.com**

Townsend Press, Inc.
1038 Industrial Drive
West Berlin, New Jersey 08091

ISBN 1-59194-001-X

Library of Congress Control Number:
2002110935

TABLE OF CONTENTS

CHAPTER 1

Into the Primitive

Buck did not read the newspapers, or he would have known that trouble was brewing, not for himself alone, but for every dog from Puget Sound to San Diego who possessed strong muscles and warm, long hair. Men groping in the Arctic darkness had found a yellow metal, and steamship and transportation companies were booming with business. Thousands of men were rushing into the Northland. These men wanted work dogs—heavy dogs with strong muscles and furry coats to protect them from the frost.

Buck lived in a big house in the sun-kissed Santa Clara Valley. It was called Judge Miller's

1

place. It stood back from the road, half-hidden among the trees, through which one could see the wide, cool veranda that ran around its four sides. The house was approached by graveled driveways that wound about through wide-spreading lawns and under the interlacing boughs of tall poplars. At the rear, things were on an even more spacious scale than at the front. There were great stables, where a dozen grooms and boys gathered; rows of vine-clad servants' cottages; an endless and orderly array of outhouses; long grape arbors, green pastures, orchards, and berry patches.

Buck ruled over this great domain. He had been born here four years ago, and had lived here all his life. There were other dogs, but they did not count. They came and went, resided in the crowded kennels, or lived unnoticed in the recesses of the house.

But Buck was neither house dog nor kennel dog. The whole realm was his. He plunged into the swimming tank or went hunting with the Judge's sons. He escorted the Judge's daughters on long twilight or early morning walks. On wintry nights he lay at the Judge's feet before the roaring library fire. He carried the Judge's grandsons on his back, or rolled them in the grass, and guarded their footsteps through wild adventures in the stable yard. He dominantly stalked among the terriers and utterly ignored the others, for he was king—king over all creeping, crawling, flying things of Judge Miller's place, humans included.

His father, Elmo, a huge St. Bernard, had been the Judge's inseparable companion, and Buck was to follow in the way of his father. He was not as large—he weighed only one hundred and forty pounds—because his mother, Shep, had been a smaller Scotch shepherd dog. Nevertheless, one hundred and forty pounds, to which was added the dignity that comes of good living and universal respect, enabled him to carry himself in royal fashion. He had a fine pride in himself. He was even a trifle egotistical, as country gentlemen sometimes become. But he was not a pampered house dog. Hunting and other outdoor delights had kept down the fat and hardened his muscles; his love of water had been a tonic and a health preserver.

This was Buck's life in the fall of 1897, when the Klondike gold rush dragged men from all the world into the frozen North. But Buck did not read the newspapers, and he did not know that Manuel, one of the gardener's helpers, was not to be trusted. Manuel had one overriding sin. He loved to gamble. But gambling requires money, and the wages of a gardener's helper did not even cover the needs of his wife and many children.

The Judge was at a meeting on the memorable night of Manuel's betrayal. No one saw him and Buck go off through the orchard on what Buck imagined was merely a stroll. And with the exception of a solitary man, no one saw them arrive at the little train station. This man talked with Manuel, and money changed hands between them.

"You might wrap up the goods before you deliver 'em," the stranger said gruffly, and Manuel doubled a piece of thick rope around Buck's neck under the collar.

"Twist it, an' you'll choke 'em plenty," said Manuel, and the stranger grunted in agreement.

Buck had accepted the rope with quiet dignity. It was surely a new experience, but he had learned to trust in men he knew, and to give them credit for wisdom beyond his own. But when the ends of the rope were placed in the stranger's hands, he growled threateningly, making his displeasure clear. But to his surprise the rope tightened around his neck, shutting off his breath. In a rage he sprang at the man, who met him halfway, grabbed him by the throat, and with a twist threw him over on his back. Then he tightened the rope without mercy, while Buck struggled in a fury, his tongue lolling out of his mouth and his great chest panting in vain. Never in all his life had he been so vilely treated, and never had he been so angry. But his strength decreased, his eyes glazed, and he knew nothing when the train stopped and the two men threw him into the baggage car.

The next he knew, he was dimly aware that his tongue was hurting and he was being jolted along in some kind of vehicle. The shriek of a locomotive whistling at a crossing told him where he was. He had traveled too often with the Judge not to know the sensation of riding in a baggage car. He opened his eyes, and into them came the unbridled anger of a kidnapped king. The man sprang for his throat, but Buck was too quick for him. His jaws closed on the hand and did not relax till the man choked his senses out of him once more.

"Yep, the dog has fits," the man said, hiding his mangled hand from the baggageman, who had been attracted by the sounds of struggle. "I'm takin' 'm up for the boss to 'Frisco. A crack dog-doctor there thinks that he can cure 'm."

Later that night, Buck was taken to a shed in back of a saloon on the San Francisco waterfront.

"All I got was fifty for it," he grumbled; "an' I wouldn't do it over again for a thousand, cold cash."

His hand was wrapped in a bloody handkerchief, and his right trouser leg was ripped from knee to ankle.

"How much did the other one get?" the saloonkeeper demanded.

"A hundred," was the reply. "Wouldn't take a cent less, so help me."

"That makes a hundred and fifty," the saloonkeeper calculated; "and I'd say he's worth it."

Dazed and suffering unbearable pain in throat and tongue, with the life half throttled out of him, Buck attempted to face his tormentors. But he was thrown down and choked repeatedly, till they succeeded in cutting the heavy brass collar off his neck. Then the rope was removed, and he was flung into a cagelike crate.

There he lay for the remainder of the weary night, nursing his rage and wounded pride. He could not understand what it all meant. What did these strange men want with him? Why were they keeping him pent up in this narrow crate? He did not know why, but he felt the vague sense of impending disaster. Several times during the night he sprang to his feet when the shed door rattled open, expecting to see the Judge, but each time it was the bulging face of the saloonkeeper that peered in at him. And each time the joyful bark that trembled in Buck's throat was twisted into a savage growl.

But he was left alone, and in the morning four men entered and picked up the crate. More tormentors, Buck decided, for they were evil-looking creatures, ragged and unkempt. He stormed and raged at them through the bars. They only laughed and poked sticks at him, which he promptly attacked with his teeth till he realized that was what they wanted. So he lay down sullenly and allowed the crate to be lifted into a wagon. Then he, and the crate in which he was imprisoned, began a passage through many hands. Finally he was deposited in the express car of the long, loud train.

For two days locomotives shrieked, and for two days and nights Buck neither ate nor drank. In his anger he had met the first advances of the train men with growls, and they retaliated by teasing him. When he flung himself against the bars, quivering and frothing, they laughed at him and taunted him. They growled and barked like wild dogs, and flapped their arms and crowed. He knew it was all very silly, but still it was an outrage to his dignity. His anger grew and grew. He did not mind the hunger so much, but the lack of water caused him severe suffering, and his wrath grew to fever pitch.

He was glad for one thing: the rope was off his neck. That had given them an unfair advantage; but now that it was off, he would show them. They would never get another rope around his neck. Upon that he was resolved. For two days and nights he neither ate nor drank, and during those days and nights of torment, his rage was building. His eyes turned bloodshot, and he evolved into a raging fiend. He was so changed that the Judge himself would not have recognized him; and the train men breathed with relief when they bundled him off the train and into a wagon at Seattle.

Four men carefully carried the crate from the wagon into a small, high-walled back yard. A stout man with a red sweater came out and signed the book for the driver. That was the man, Buck decided, the next tormentor, and he hurled himself savagely against the bars. The man smiled grimly and brought a hatchet and a club.

"You ain't going to take him out now?" the driver asked.

"Sure," the man replied, driving the hatchet into the crate.

There was an instantaneous scattering of the four men who had carried it in, and from safe perches on top the wall they prepared to watch the performance.

Buck rushed at the splintering wood, sinking his teeth into it, surging and wrestling with it. Wherever the hatchet fell on the outside, he was there on the inside, snarling and growling. He was as furiously anxious to get out as the man in the red sweater was calmly intent on getting him out.

"Now, you red-eyed devil," he said, when he had made an opening sufficient for the passage of Buck's body. At the same time he dropped the hatchet and shifted the club to his right hand.

And Buck was truly a red-eyed devil, ready to spring, hair bristling, mouth foaming, a mad glitter in his bloodshot eyes. He launched his one hundred and forty pounds of fury straight at the man, surcharged with the pent-up passion of two days and nights. In mid-air, just as his jaws were about to close on the man, he received a shock to his body and brought his teeth together with an agonizing clip. He whirled over, hitting the ground on his back and side. He had never been struck by a club in his life, and he did not understand. With a snarl that was part bark and more scream, he was again on his feet and launched into the air. And again the shock came, and he was brought crushingly to the ground. This time he was aware that it was the club, but his madness knew no caution. A dozen times he charged, and as often the club broke the charge and smashed him down.

After a particularly fierce blow, he crawled to his feet too dazed to rush. He staggered limply about, the blood flowing from nose and mouth and ears, his beautiful coat sprayed and flecked with blood. Then the man advanced and deliberately dealt him a frightful blow on the nose. All the pain he had endured was as nothing compared with the agony of this. With a roar that was almost lionlike in its ferociousness, he again hurled himself at the man. But the man, shifting the club from right to left, coolly caught him by the under jaw, at the same time wrenching downward and backward. Buck was thrown up in the air; then he crashed to the ground on his head and chest.

For the last time he rushed. The man struck the blow he had purposely withheld for so long, and Buck crumpled up and went down, knocked utterly senseless.

"He's no slouch at dog-breakin', that's

wot I say," one of the men on the wall cried out enthusiastically.

Buck's senses came back to him, but not his strength. He lay where he had fallen, and from there he watched the man in the red sweater.

"'Answers to the name of Buck,'" the man read from the saloon-keeper's letter, which had announced the crate and contents. "Well, Buck, my boy," he went on in a friendly voice, "we've had our little quarrel, and the best thing we can do is to let it go at that. You've learned your place, and I know mine. Be a good dog and all will go well. Be a bad dog, and I'll whale the stuffin' outa you. Understand?"

As he spoke, he fearlessly patted the head he had so mercilessly pounded, and though Buck's hair involuntarily bristled at the touch of his hand, he endured it without protest. When the man brought him water, he drank eagerly, and later bolted down a generous meal of raw meat, chunk by chunk, from the man's hand.

He was beaten (he knew that); but he was not broken. He saw, once and for all, that he stood no chance against a man with a club. He had learned this lesson, and he never forgot it. It was his introduction to the reign of primitive law. The facts of life took on a fiercer aspect, and while he faced it unintimidated, he faced it with all the hidden cunning of his natural instincts aroused. As the days went by, other dogs came, in crates and at the ends of ropes, some quietly, and some raging and roaring as he had come. One after the other, he watched them pass under the domination of the man in the red sweater. Again and again, as he watched each brutal performance, the lesson was driven home to Buck: a man with a club was a lawgiver, a master to be obeyed, though not necessarily accepted. Of this Buck was never guilty, though he did see beaten dogs that fawned upon the man, and wagged their tails, and licked his hand. Also he saw one dog that would neither appease nor obey finally killed in the struggle for mastery.

Now and again men came, strangers, who talked excitedly to the man in the red sweater. And at times that money passed between them, the strangers took one or more of the dogs away with them. Buck wondered where they went, for they never came back. But the fear of the future was strong upon him, and he was glad each time when he was not selected.

Yet his time came, in the form of a little shriveled man who spoke broken English and had many strange expressions that Buck could not understand.

"Sacredam!" he cried, when his eyes lit upon Buck. "Dat one dam bully dog! Eh? How moch?"

"Three hundred, and a present at that, eh, Perrault?" was the prompt reply of the man in the red sweater.

Perrault grinned. Considering that the price of dogs had boomed skyward by the unusual demand, it was not an unfair sum for so fine an animal. And Perrault knew dogs, and when he looked at Buck he knew that he was one in a thousand—"One in ten t'ousand," he commented mentally.

Buck saw money pass between them and was not surprised when Curly, a good-natured Newfoundland, and he were led away by the little man. That was the last he saw of the man in the red sweater, and as he and Curly looked at receding Seattle from the deck of the Narwhal, it was the last he saw of the warm Southland. Curly and he were taken below by Perrault and turned over to a black-faced giant called Francois. They were a new kind of men to Buck, and while he developed no affection for them, he nonetheless grew to honestly respect them. He speedily learned that Perrault and Francois were fair men, calm and impartial in administering justice, and wise in the way of dogs.

On the deck of the Narwhal, Buck and Curly joined two other dogs. One of them was a big snow-white fellow named Spitz. He was friendly, in a treacherous sort of way, smiling into one's face while he planned some under-handed trick. For instance, he stole from Buck's food at the first meal. As Buck sprang to pun-ish him, the lash of Francois's whip sang through the air, reaching the culprit first; and nothing remained for Buck but to recover the bone. That was fair of Francois, he decided, and Francois began his rise in Buck's estimation.

The other dog made no advances nor received any. He did not attempt to steal from the newcomers. He was a gloomy fellow, and he showed Curly plainly that all he desired was to be left alone. His name was Dave, and he ate and slept and took interest in nothing, not even when the ship crossed Queen Charlotte Sound and rolled and pitched and bucked like a thing possessed. When Buck and Curly grew excited, half wild with fear, he raised his head as though annoyed, favored them with a glance, yawned, and went to sleep again.

Day and night the ship throbbed to the tireless pulse of the propeller, and though one day was very like another, it was apparent to Buck that the weather was steadily growing colder. At last, one morning, the propeller was quiet, and the Narwhal was filled with an atmosphere of excitement. He felt it, as did the other dogs, and knew that a change was at hand. Francois leashed them and brought them on deck. At the first step upon the cold surface, Buck's feet sank into something white and mushy—very much like mud. He sprang back with a snort. More of this white stuff was falling through the air. He shook himself, but more of it fell upon him. He sniffed it curiously, then licked some up on his tongue. It bit like fire, and the next instant it was gone. This puzzled him. He tried it again with the same result. The onlookers laughed uproariously. He didn't know why, and he felt ashamed. This was his first snow.

CHAPTER 2
The Law of Club and Fang

Buck's first day on land was like a night-mare. Every hour was filled with shock and surprise. He had been suddenly jerked from the heart of civilization and flung into the heart of things primordial. There was no peace, no rest, and not a moment's safety. All was confusion and action, and every moment life and limb were in peril. It was crucial to be constantly alert, for these dogs and men were savages, all of them, who knew no law but the law of club and fang.

He had never seen dogs fight as these wolfish creatures fought, and his first experi-ence taught him an unforgettable lesson.

Curly was the victim. They were camped near the log store, where she, in her friendly way, made advances to a husky dog the size of a full-grown wolf, though not half so large as she. There was no warning, only a leap, a clip of teeth, and Curly's face was ripped open from eye to jaw.

This was the way wolves fight—to strike and leap away; but there was more to it than this. Thirty or forty huskies ran to the spot and surrounded the combatants in an intent and silent circle. Buck did not comprehend that silent intentness, nor the eagerness with which they were licking their chops. Curly rushed her attacker, who struck again and leaped aside. He met her next rush with his chest and tumbled her off her feet. She never regained them. This was what the onlooking huskies had waited for. They closed in upon her, snarling and yelping; and she was buried, screaming with agony, beneath the bristling mass of bodies.

It was so sudden, and so unexpected, that Buck was taken aback. He saw Spitz run out his bloody tongue in a way he had of laughing; and he saw Francois, swinging an axe, spring into the mess of dogs. Three men with clubs were helping him to scatter them. It did not take long. Two minutes from the time Curly went down, the last of her attackers was clubbed off. But she lay there limp and lifeless in the bloody, trampled snow, almost literally torn to pieces. The scene often came back to Buck to trouble him in his sleep. So that was the way. No fair play. Once down, that was the end of you. Well, he would see to it that he never went down. Spitz ran out his tongue and laughed again, and from that moment Buck hated him with a bitter and undying hatred.

Before he had recovered from the shock of the tragic passing of Curly, he received another shock. Francois fastened upon him an arrangement of straps and buckles. It was a harness, such as he had seen the grooms put on the horses at home. And as he had seen horses work, so he was set to work, hauling Francois on a sled to the forest that fringed the valley, and returning with a load of firewood. Though his dignity was sorely hurt, he was too wise to rebel. He buckled down and did his best, though it was all new and strange. Francois was stern, demanding instant obedience, and by virtue of his whip receiving instant obedience. Dave, who was an experienced sled dog, nipped Buck's hindquarters whenever he was in error. Spitz was the leader, likewise experienced, and while he could not always get at Buck, he growled sharp reproof now and again, or cleverly threw his weight in the traces to jerk Buck into the way he should go. Buck learned easily and made remarkable progress. When they returned to camp, he knew enough to stop at "ho," to go ahead at "mush," to swing wide on the bends, and to stay clear when the loaded sled shot downhill at their heels.

"T'ree very good dogs," Francois told Perrault. "Dat Buck, heem pool lak hell. I tich heem queek as anyt'ing."

By afternoon, Perrault, who was in a hurry to be on the trail, returned with two more dogs. "Billee" and "Joe" he called them, two brothers, and true huskies both. Though they were sons of one mother, they were as different as day and night. Billee's one fault was his excessive good nature, while Joe was the very opposite, sour and introspective, with a constant snarl. Buck received them in a friendly fashion, Dave ignored them, while Spitz proceeded to thrash first one and then the other. Billee wagged his tail appeasingly, turned to run when he saw that appeasement was of no use, and cried when Spitz's sharp teeth cut into his flank. But no matter how Spitz circled, Joe whirled around on his heels to face him, mane bristling, ears laid back, lips writhing and snarling, jaws clipping together as fast as he could snap, and eyes devilishly gleaming. His appearance was so terrible that Spitz was forced to forgo disciplining him. But to cover his own discomfort he turned upon the inoffensive and wailing Billee and drove him to the confines of the camp.

By evening Perrault secured another dog, an old husky, long and lean and gaunt, with a battle-scarred face and a single eye which flashed a warning of prowess that commanded respect. He was called Sol-leks, which means "the Angry One." Like Dave, he asked nothing, gave nothing, expected nothing. When he marched slowly and deliberately into their midst, even Spitz left him alone. He had one peculiarity that Buck was unlucky enough to discover. He did not like to be approached on his blind side. Buck was unwittingly guilty of this offense. The first knowledge he had of his indiscretion was when Sol-leks whirled upon him and slashed his shoulder to the bone. Forever after, Buck avoided his blind side and had no more trouble. His only apparent ambition, like Dave's, was to be left alone.

That night Buck faced the great problem of sleeping. The tent, illumined by a candle, glowed warmly in the midst of the white plain. When he, as a matter of course, entered it, both Perrault and Francois bombarded him with curses and cooking utensils till he fled out into the cold. A chill wind was blowing that nipped him sharply and bit with particular venom into his wounded shoulder. He lay down on the snow and attempted to sleep, but the frost soon drove him shivering to his feet. Miserable and alone, he wandered about among the many tents only to find that one place was as cold as another. Here and there savage dogs rushed upon him, but he bristled his neck-hair and snarled (for he was learning fast), and they let him go his way unmolested.

Finally an idea came to him. He would return and see how his own teammates were making out. To his astonishment, they had disappeared. Again he wandered about through the great camp, looking for them, and again he returned. Were they in the tent? No, that could not be, or he would not have been driven out. Then where could they possibly be? With drooping tail and shivering body, very forlorn indeed, he aimlessly circled the tent. Suddenly the snow gave way beneath his forelegs and he sank down. Something wriggled under his feet. He sprang back, bristling and snarling, fearful of the unseen and unknown. But a friendly little yelp reassured him, and he went back to investigate. A whiff of warm air ascended to his nostrils, and there, curled up under the snow in a snug ball, lay

Billee. He whined assuringly, squirmed and wriggled to show his good will and intentions, and even ventured, as a bribe for peace, to lick Buck's face with his warm, wet tongue.

Another lesson. So that was the way they did it, eh? Buck confidently selected a spot and proceeded to dig a hole for himself. In an instant, the heat from his body filled the confined space, and he was asleep. The day had been long and tiring, and he slept soundly and comfortably, though he growled and barked and wrestled with bad dreams.

He did not open his eyes till roused by the noises of the waking camp. At first he did not know where he was. It had snowed during the night, and he was completely buried. The snow walls pressed him on every side, and a great surge of fear swept through him—the instinctive fear of the wild animal for the trap. The muscles of his whole body contracted instinctively, the hair on his neck and shoulders stood on end, and with a ferocious snarl he bounded straight up into the blinding day, the snow flying about him in a flashing cloud. He landed on his feet and saw the white camp spread out before him. He knew where he was and remembered all that had passed from the time he went for a stroll with Manuel to the hole he had dug for himself the night before.

A shout from Francois hailed his appearance. "Wot I say?" the dog-driver cried to Perrault. "Dat Buck for sure learn queek as anyt'ing."

Perrault nodded gravely. As courier for the Canadian government, carrying important mail, he was anxious to secure the best dogs, and he was particularly pleased by the possession of Buck.

Three more huskies were added to the team inside an hour, making a total of nine, and before another quarter of an hour had passed, they were in harness and swinging up the trail. Buck was glad to be gone, and though the work was hard, he found he did not particularly despise it. He was surprised at the eagerness which animated the whole team and which was communicated to him. Even more surprising was the change in Dave and Sol-leks. They were new dogs, utterly transformed by the harness. All passiveness had dropped from them. They were alert and active, anxious that the work should go well, and fiercely irritable with whatever, by delay or confusion, slowed that work. The toil of the traces seemed the supreme expression of their being, and all that they lived for, the only thing in which they took delight.

Dave was wheeler or sled dog; pulling in

front of him was Buck; then came Sol-leks. The rest of the team was strung out ahead, single file, to the leader, whose position was filled by Spitz.

Buck had been purposely placed between Dave and Sol-leks so that he might receive instruction. He was an apt scholar, and they were equally apt teachers, never allowing him to linger long in error, and enforcing their teaching with their sharp teeth. Dave was fair and very wise. He never nipped Buck without cause, and he never failed to nip him when he was in need of it. As Francois's whip backed him up, Buck found it to be better to mend his ways than to retaliate. Once, during a brief halt, when he got tangled in the traces and delayed the start, both Dave and Sol-leks flew at him and administered a sound trouncing. The resulting tangle was even worse, but Buck took good care to keep the traces clear thereafter. When the day was done, he had mastered his work so well that his mates stopped nagging him. Francois's whip snapped less frequently, and Perrault even honored Buck by lifting up his feet and carefully examining them.

It was a hard day's run across glaciers and snowdrifts hundreds of feet deep. They made good time down the chain of lakes that filled the craters of extinct volcanoes, and late that night they pulled into a huge camp, where thousands of goldseekers were building boats to prepare for the breakup of the ice in the spring. Buck made his hole in the snow and slept the sleep of the exhausted, but all too early he was rousted out in the cold darkness and harnessed with his mates to the sled.

That day they traveled forty miles, the trail being packed; but the next day, and for many days to follow, they broke their own trail, worked harder, and made poorer time. As a rule, Perrault traveled ahead of the team, packing the snow with webbed shoes to make it easier for them. Francois, guiding the sled, sometimes exchanged places with him, but not often. Perrault was in a hurry, and he prided himself on his indispensable knowledge of ice, for the fall ice was very thin, and where there was swift water, there was no ice at all.

Day after day, for days unending, Buck toiled in the traces. Always, they broke camp in the dark, and they hit the trail at the first gray of dawn. And always they pitched camp after dark, eating their bit of fish, and crawling to sleep into the snow. Buck was ravenous. The pound and a half of sun-dried salmon, which was his ration for each day, seemed to go nowhere. He never had enough and suffered from perpetual hunger pangs. Yet the other dogs, because they weighed less and were born to this life, received only a pound of the fish and managed to keep in good condition.

He swiftly lost the neatness and care which had characterized his old life. A dainty eater, he found that his mates, finishing first, robbed him of his unfinished ration. There was no defending it. While he was fighting off two or three, it was disappearing down the throats of the others. To remedy this, he ate as fast as they did; and he was so hungry that he was not above taking what did not belong to him. He watched and learned. When he saw Pike, one of the new dogs, a clever thief, slyly steal a slice of bacon when Perrault's back was turned, he duplicated the performance the following day, getting away with the whole chunk. A great uproar was raised, but he was unsuspected; while Dub, an awkward blunderer who was always getting caught, was punished for Buck's misdeed.

This first theft showed Buck was fit to survive in the hostile Northland environment. It marked his adaptability, his capacity to adjust himself to changing conditions, the lack of which would have meant swift and terrible death. It marked, further, the decay of his moral nature, which was a handicap in the ruthless struggle for existence. It was all well enough in the Southland, under the law of love and fellowship, to respect private property and personal feelings. But in the Northland, under the law of club and fang, one who took such things into account was a fool and would fail to prosper.

Not that Buck reasoned it out, but unconsciously he accommodated himself to this new mode of life. All his days, no matter what the odds, he had never run from a fight. But the club of the man in the red sweater had beaten into him a more fundamental and primitive code. Civilized, he would have died for a moral consideration, say the defense of Judge Miller. But the complete loss of his civilization was now clear in his ability to flee from any moral consideration to save his hide. He did not steal for joy of it, but because of his hunger. He did not rob openly, but stole secretly and cunningly, out of respect for club and fang.

His regression was rapid. His muscles became hard as iron, and he grew callous to all ordinary pain. He could eat anything, no matter how loathsome or indigestible; and, once he had eaten, the juices of his stomach extracted the least particle of nutrition; and his blood carried it to the farthest reaches of his body, building it into the toughest tissues. His sight and scent became remarkably keen, while his hearing developed such acuteness that in his sleep he heard the faintest sound and knew whether it meant peace or peril. He learned to bite the ice out with his teeth when it collected between his toes. When he was thirsty and there was a thick scum of ice over the water hole, he would break it by rearing and striking it with his legs. His most notable trait was an ability to scent the wind and forecast it a night in advance. No matter how still the air when he dug his nest by tree or bank, the wind that later blew inevitably found him sheltered and snug.

And not only did he learn by experience, but instincts long dead became alive again. The generations of domestication fell away from him. In vague ways he remembered back to the youth of his breed, to the time wild dogs ranged in packs and killed their meat as they ran it down. It was no task for him to learn to fight with cut and slash and the quick wolf snap. His forgotten ancestors had fought in this manner. They activated the old life instinctively within him, and the old tricks of his breed became his tricks. They came to him without effort or discovery, as though they had always been his. And when, on the still, cold nights, he pointed his nose at a star and howled long and wolflike, it was his ancestors, dead and dust, pointing nose at star and howling down through the centuries and through him.

CHAPTER 3

The Dominant Primordial Beast

The dominant primordial beast was strong in Buck, and under the fierce conditions of life on the trail, it grew and grew. Yet it was a secret growth. His newborn cunning gave him poise and control. He was too busy adjusting himself to this new life to feel at ease. Not only did he not pick fights, but he avoided them whenever possible. His attitude was deliberate. He did not make sudden moves, and in spite of the bitter hatred between him and Spitz, he showed no impatience and avoided all offensive acts.

On the other hand, possibly because he sensed that Buck was a dangerous rival, Spitz never lost an opportunity to show his teeth. He even went out of his way to bully Buck, striving constantly to start the fight which could end only in the death of one or the other.

Early in the trip this might have taken place, had it not been for an unusual accident. At the end of this day they made a bleak and miserable camp on the shore of Lake Le Barge. Driving snow, a wind that cut like a white-hot knife, and darkness had forced them to find a camping place. The place they found could hardly have been worse. At their backs rose a wall of rock, and Perrault and Francois were forced to make their fire and spread their sleeping robes on the ice of the lake itself. They had discarded the tent in order to travel light. A few sticks of driftwood furnished them with a fire that thawed down through the ice and left them to eat supper in the dark.

Buck made his nest under the sheltering rock. It was so snug and warm that he didn't want to leave it when Francois distributed the fish. But when Buck finished his ration and returned, he found his nest occupied. A warning snarl told him that the trespasser was Spitz. Till now Buck had avoided trouble with his enemy, but this was too much. The beast in him roared. He sprang upon Spitz with a fury that surprised them both. Spitz was particularly surprised. For his whole experience with Buck had led him to believe that his rival was an unusually timid dog, who held his own only because of his great weight and size.

Francois was surprised, too, when they came shooting out of the nest in a tangle and he realized the cause of the trouble. "A-a- ah!" he cried to Buck. "Gif it to heem, by Gar! Gif it to heem, the dirty t'eef!"

Spitz was equally willing. He was crying with sheer rage and eagerness as he circled back and forth for a chance to spring in. Buck was no less eager, and no less cautious, as he likewise circled back and forth for the advantage. But it was then that the unexpected happened, the thing that took their struggle for power to the next level.

A shout from Perrault, the resounding impact of a club upon a bony frame, and a shrill yelp of pain, announced the uproar. The camp was suddenly alive with dozens of starving huskies, who had scented the camp from some Indian village. They had crept in while Buck and Spitz were fighting. When the two men sprang among them with clubs, they showed their teeth and fought back. They were crazed by the smell of the food. Perrault found one with his head buried in the foodbox. His club landed heavily on the gaunt ribs, and the box was turned over on the ground. In an instant a dozen starving dogs were scrambling for the bread and bacon. The clubs fell upon them unheeded. They yelped and howled under the rain of blows, but struggled nonetheless madly till the last crumb had been devoured.

In the meantime the astonished teamdogs had burst out of their nests, only to be attacked by the fierce invaders. Never had Buck seen such dogs. They were mere skeletons with blazing eyes and shining fangs. But their hunger-madness made them terrifying. The teamdogs were swept back against the cliff at the first onset. Buck was beset by three huskies, and in an instant his head and shoulders were ripped and slashed. The din was frightful. Billee was crying as usual. Dave and Sol-leks, dripping blood from scores of wounds, were fighting bravely side by side. Joe was snapping like a demon. His teeth closed on the leg of a husky, and he crunched down through the bone. Pike leaped upon the crippled animal, breaking its neck with a quick flash of teeth. Buck got a wild adversary by the throat and was sprayed with blood when his teeth sank through the jugular. The warm taste of it in his mouth urged him to greater fierceness. He flung himself upon another, and at the same time felt teeth sink into his own throat. It was Spitz, treacherously attacking from the side.

Perrault and Francois hurried to save their sled dogs. When the two men ran back to save the food, the wild huskies returned to the attack on the team. Billee, terrified into bravery, sprang through the savage circle and fled away over the ice. Pike and Dub followed on his heels, with the rest of the team behind. As Buck drew himself together to spring after them, out of the tail of his eye he saw Spitz rush upon him. Once off his feet and under that mass of huskies, there was no hope for him. But he braced himself to the shock of Spitz's charge, then joined the flight out onto the lake.

Later, the nine teamdogs gathered together and sought shelter in the forest. Though unpursued, they were in a sorry state. All were wounded, some seriously. Dub was badly injured in a hind leg; Dolly, the last husky added to the team, had a torn throat; Joe had lost an eye; while Billee, with an ear chewed to ribbons, cried and whimpered throughout the night. At daybreak they limped warily back to camp to find the marauders gone and the two men in bad tempers. Half their food supply was gone. The huskies had chewed through the sled lashings and canvas coverings. In fact, nothing, no matter how remotely edible, had escaped them. They had eaten a pair of Perrault's moose-hide moccasins, chunks out of the leather traces, and even two feet of lash from the end of Francois's whip. He broke from the sorrowful thought of it to look over his wounded dogs.

"Ah, my frien's," he said softly, "mebbe it mek you mad dog, dose many bites. Mebbe all mad dog, sacredam! Wot you t'ink, eh, Perrault?"

Perrault shook his head. With four hundred miles of trail still ahead, he could not afford to have madness break out among his dogs. Two hours of cursing and hard work got the harnesses into shape, and the wounded team was under way, struggling painfully over the hardest part of the trail they had yet encountered.

The Thirty Mile River was wide open. Its wild water defied the frost. Six days of exhausting toil were required to cover those thirty terrible miles. Every foot along the way put the lives of the men and dogs at risk. A dozen times, Perrault, leading the way, broke through the ice, saving himself by the long pole he carried. But a cold snap was on, the thermometer registering fifty below zero, and each time he broke the ice, he was forced to build a fire and dry his garments or risk his life.

Nothing discouraged Perrault. He took any risk, purposefully thrusting his worn little face into the frost and struggling on from dawn to dark. He risked walking out on ice that bent and crackled underfoot and upon which they dared not pause. Once, the sled with Dave and Buck broke through the ice, and they were half-frozen and all but drowned by the time they were dragged out. The usual fire was necessary to save them. They were solidly coated with ice, and the two men kept them on the run around the fire, sweating and thawing, so close that they were singed by the flames.

Another time Spitz broke through, dragging the whole team with him up to Buck, who strained backward with all his strength, his forepaws on the slippery edge and the ice quivering and snapping all around. But behind him was Dave, likewise straining backward, and behind the sled was Francois, pulling with all his might.

Again, the ice broke away before and behind, and there was no escape except up a cliff. Perrault scaled it by a miracle, while Francois prayed for just that miracle. With every last bit of harness tied into a long rope, the dogs were hoisted, one by one, to the crest of the cliff. Francois came up last, after the sled and load. Then came the search for a place to descend. The descent was ultimately made by the aid of the rope, and night found them back on the river with a quarter of a mile to the day's credit.

By the time they reached good ice, Buck and the rest of the dogs were worn out. But Perrault, to make up lost time, pushed them late and early.

Buck's feet were not so compact and hard as the feet of the huskies. His had softened during the many generations since the day his last wild ancestor was tamed. All day long he limped in agony, and once camp was made, he lay down like a dead dog. Hungry as he was, he would not move to receive his ration of fish, which Francois had to bring to him. He also rubbed Buck's feet for half an hour each night after supper, and he sacrificed the tops of his own moccasins to make four moccasins for Buck. This was a great relief, and Buck caused even Perrault's face to twist itself into a grin one morning, when Francois forgot the moccasins and Buck lay on his back, his four feet waving in the air, refusing to budge without them. Later his feet grew hard to the trail, and the worn-out footgear was thrown away.

One morning, as they were harnessing up, Dolly, who had never been noticeable for any reason, went suddenly mad. She announced her condition by a long, heartbreaking wolf howl that sent every dog bristling with fear. Then she sprang straight for Buck. He had never seen a dog go mad, yet he knew that here was horror and fled away from it in a panic. He raced straight away, with Dolly, panting and frothing, one leap behind. His terror was so great that she could not gain on him; nor could he lose her, so great was her madness. He plunged through the wooded center of the island, flew down to the lower end, crossed a back channel filled with rough ice to another island, gained a third island, curved back to the main river, and in desperation started to cross it. And all the time, though he did not look, he could hear her snarling just one leap behind. Francois called to him a quarter of a mile away, and he doubled back, still one leap ahead, gasping painfully for air and putting all his faith in Francois to save him. The dog-driver held the axe poised in his hand, and as Buck shot past him, the axe crashed down upon mad Dolly's head.

Buck staggered over against the sled, exhausted, sobbing for breath, helpless. This was Spitz's opportunity. He sprang upon

Buck, and sank his teeth into his unresisting foe and ripped and tore the flesh to the bone. Then Francois's lash descended, and Buck had the satisfaction of watching Spitz receive the worst whipping as yet administered to any of the team.

"One devil, dat Spitz," remarked Perrault. "Some dam day heem keel dat Buck."

"Dat Buck two devils," was Francois's response. "All de time I watch dat Buck I know for sure. Lissen: some dam fine day heem get mad lak hell an' den heem chew dat Spitz all up and spit heem out on de snow. Sure. I know."

From then on it was war between them. Spitz, as lead-dog and acknowledged master of the team, felt his supremacy threatened by this strange Southland dog. Buck was strange to him, for of the many Southland dogs he had known, not one had shown himself worthy in camp and on the trail. They were all too soft, dying under the toil, the frost, and starvation. Buck was the exception. He alone endured and prospered, matching the husky in strength, savagery, and cunning. He was a masterful dog, and what made him dangerous was the fact that the club of the man in the red sweater had knocked all recklessness out of him. He was sly and could bide his time with a patience that was nothing less than primitive.

It was inevitable that the clash for leadership should come. Buck wanted it. He wanted it because it was his nature, because he had been gripped by an incomprehensible pride— that pride which keeps dogs toiling down to their last gasp, which lures them to die joyfully in the harness and breaks their hearts if they are cut out of the harness. This was the pride of Dave as wheel-dog, of Sol-leks as he pulled with all his strength; the pride that transformed them from sour, sullen brutes into eager, ambitious creatures. The pride that spurred them on all day and dropped them as camp was pitched at night. This was the pride that made Spitz thrash the sleddogs who blundered or hid away at harness-up time in the morning. Likewise it was this pride that made him fear Buck as a possible lead-dog. And this was Buck's pride, too.

He openly threatened the other's leadership. One night there was a heavy snowfall, and in the morning Pike did not appear. He was securely hidden in his nest under a foot of snow. Francois called him in vain. Spitz was wild with anger. He raged through the camp, smelling and digging in every likely place, snarling so frightfully that Pike heard and shivered in his hiding-place.

But when he was at last unearthed, and Spitz flew at him to punish him, Buck flew, with equal rage, between them. It was so unexpected, and so shrewdly managed, that Spitz was hurled backward and off his feet. Pike, who had been trembling with fear, took heart at this open mutiny and sprang upon his overthrown leader. Buck, to whom fair play was a forgotten code, likewise sprang upon Spitz. But Francois, chuckling at the incident, was still unswerving in the administration of justice. He brought his lash down upon Buck with all his might. This failed to drive Buck from his fallen rival, and the butt of the whip was brought into play. Half-stunned by the blow, Buck was knocked backward and the lash laid upon him again and again, while Spitz soundly punished the offending Pike.

In the days that followed, as Dawson drew closer and closer, Buck still continued to interfere between Spitz and the culprits; but he did it craftily, when Francois was not around. With the hidden mutiny of Buck, a general disregard for authority sprang up and increased. Dave and Sol-leks were unaffected, but the rest of the team went from bad to worse. Things no longer went right. There was continual bickering. Trouble was always afoot, and at the bottom of it was Buck. He kept Francois busy, for the dog-driver was just waiting for the life-and-death struggle between the two which he knew must take place sooner or later. On more than one night he was up from his sleep at the sounds of quarreling and strife among the other dogs, fearful that Buck and Spitz were at it.

But the opportunity did not present itself, and they pulled into Dawson one dreary afternoon with the great fight still to come. Here were many men and countless dogs, and Buck found them all at work. It seemed the natural order of things that dogs should work. All day they swung up and down the main street in long teams, and in the night their jingling bells still went by. They hauled cabin logs and firewood and did all manner of work that horses did in the Santa Clara Valley. Here and there Buck met Southland dogs, but mainly they were the wild wolf husky breed. Every night, they lifted their voices in song, a weird and eerie chant, in which it was Buck's delight to join.

Seven days from the time they pulled into Dawson, they dropped down the steep bank by the Barracks to the Yukon Trail. Perrault was carrying mail, and the pride of travel had gripped him. He wanted to make the record trip of the year. Several things were in his favor.

The week's rest had revived them. The trail was packed hard. And the police had arranged for deposits of food for dog and man in two or three places. And he was traveling light.

They made a fifty-mile run on the first day, and the second day saw them booming up the Yukon. But such splendid running was achieved with great trouble. The underlying revolt led by Buck had destroyed the solidarity of the team. It no longer was as one dog leaping in the traces. The encouragement Buck gave the rebels led them into all kinds of petty misdemeanors. No more was Spitz a leader greatly to be feared. The old awe was gone, and they challenged his authority. Pike robbed him of half a fish one night and gulped it down under the protection of Buck. Another night Dub and Joe fought Spitz and made him forego the punishment they deserved. Buck never came near Spitz without snarling and bristling menacingly. In fact, his conduct approached that of a bully, and he was given to strutting up and down before Spitz's very nose.

The breaking down of discipline also affected the dogs in their relations with one another. They quarreled more than ever among themselves, till at times the camp was a howling bedlam. Dave and Sol-leks alone were unaltered, though they were made irritable by the unending squabbling. Francois swore and stamped the snow in futile rage. His lash was always singing among the dogs, but it was of small avail. As soon as his back was turned, they were at it again. He backed up Spitz with his whip, while Buck backed up the remainder of the team. Francois knew he was behind all the trouble, and Buck knew he knew; but Buck was too clever to be caught red-handed again. He worked faithfully in the harness, for the toil had become a delight to him; yet it was a greater delight to slyly cause a fight among his mates.

One night after supper, Dub chased a rabbit and missed. In a second the whole team was in full cry. Fifty huskies, from a camp a hundred yards away, joined the chase. The rabbit sped down the river, turned off into a small creek, and fled up the frozen bed. It ran lightly on the surface of the snow, while the dogs plowed through by mere strength. Buck led the pack, sixty strong, around bend after bend, but he could not gain. His splendid body flashed forward, leap by leap, in the wan white moonlight. And leap by leap the rabbit flashed on ahead.

The stirring of old instincts, which drives men out from the cities to the forests to hunt and kill, the blood lust, the joy of the kill—all this was Buck's, only it was infinitely more intimate. He was charging at the head of the pack, chasing the wild rabbit, the living meat, to kill with his own teeth and wash his muzzle in warm blood.

There is an ecstasy that comes when one is most alive. And it came to Buck, leading the pack, sounding the old wolf-cry, straining after the food that was alive and that fled swiftly before him through the moonlight.

He was in touch with a part of his nature that was deeper than he. He was mastered by the sheer surging of life—the tidal wave of being—the perfect joy of each muscle and joint—aglow with life, expressing itself in movement, flying jubilantly under the stars.

But Spitz, always cold and calculating, left the pack and cut across a narrow neck of land where the creek made a long bend around. As Buck rounded the bend, the rabbit still flitting before him, he saw another and larger shape leap into the immediate path of the rabbit. It was Spitz. The rabbit could not turn, and as the white teeth broke its back in mid-air, it shrieked as loudly as a stricken man may shriek, the cry of Life plunging to the grip of Death.

Buck did not cry out. He drove in upon Spitz, shoulder to shoulder, so hard that he missed his throat. They rolled over and over in the powdery snow. Spitz gained his feet, slashing Buck down the shoulder and leaping clear. Twice his teeth clipped together, like the steel jaws of a trap, as he backed away for better footing, with lips that writhed and snarled.

In a flash Buck knew it. The time had come. It was to the death. As they circled about, snarling, ears laid back, keenly watchful for the advantage, the scene came to Buck with a sense of familiarity. He seemed to remember it all—the white woods and earth, and moonlight, and the thrill of battle. Over the whiteness and silence hung a ghostly calm. There was not the faintest whisper of air— nothing moved; not a leaf quivered; the visible breaths of the dogs rose slowly and lingered in the frosty air. They had quickly finished off the rabbit, and were now drawn up in an expectant circle. They, too, were silent, their eyes gleaming and their breaths drifting slowly upward. To Buck it was nothing new or strange, this scene of a time gone by. It was as though it had always been, the expected way of things.

Spitz was a practiced fighter. His rage was bitter, but never blind. In his passion to destroy, he never forgot that his enemy was in like passion. He never rushed till he was prepared to receive a rush; never attacked till he was prepared to defend against that attack.

In vain Buck strove to sink his teeth in the neck of the big white dog. Wherever his fangs struck for the softer flesh, they were countered by the fangs of Spitz. Fang clashed against fang, and lips were cut and bleeding, but Buck could not penetrate his enemy's guard. Then he warmed up and enveloped Spitz in a whirlwind of rushes. Time and time again he tried for the snow-white throat, and every time Spitz slashed him and got away. Then Buck took to rushing, as though for the throat, but at the last moment, turning his head and ramming Spitz's shoulder with his own, trying to overthrow him. But instead, Buck's shoulder was slashed down each time as Spitz leaped lightly away.

Spitz was untouched, while Buck was streaming with blood and panting hard. The fight was growing desperate. And all the while the silent and wolfish circle waited to finish off whichever dog went down. As Buck grew winded, Spitz took to rushing in, and he kept him staggering for footing. Once Buck fell over, and the whole circle of sixty dogs started toward him, but he recovered himself, and the circle sank down again and waited.

But Buck possessed a quality that made for

greatness—imagination. He fought by instinct, but he could fight using his head as well. He rushed, as though attempting the old shoulder trick, but at the last instant swept down low to the snow. His teeth closed on Spitz's left foreleg. There was a crunch of breaking bone, and the white dog faced him on three legs. Again he tried to knock him over, then repeated the trick and broke the right foreleg. Despite the pain and helplessness, Spitz struggled madly to keep up. He saw the silent circle, with gleaming eyes, lolling tongues, and silvery breaths drifting upward, closing in upon him as he had seen similar circles close in upon beaten antagonists in the past. Only this time he was the one who was beaten.

There was no hope for him. Buck was unstoppable. Mercy was a thing reserved for gentler times. He made the final rush. The circle tightened till he could feel the breaths of the huskies on his flanks. He could see them, beyond Spitz and to either side, half crouching, ready to spring, their eyes fixed upon him. Every animal was motionless as though turned to stone. Only Spitz quivered and bristled as he staggered back and forth, snarling with horrible menace, as though to frighten off impending death. Then Buck sprang in, and shoulder at last squarely met shoulder. The dark circle became a dot on the moon-flooded snow as Spitz disappeared from view. Buck stood and looked on, the successful champion, the dominant primordial beast who had made his kill.

CHAPTER 4

Who Has Won to Mastership

"Eh? Wot I say? I spik true w'en I say dat Buck two devils. Dat Spitz fight lak hell," said Perrault, as he surveyed the gaping rips and cuts.

"An' dat Buck fight lak two hells," was Francois's answer. "An' now we make good time. No more Spitz, no more trouble, sure."

While Perrault packed the camp and loaded the sled, Francois proceeded to harness the dogs. Buck trotted up to the place Spitz would have occupied as leader, but Francois, not noticing him, brought Sol-leks to the coveted position. In his judgment, Sol-leks was the best lead-dog left. Buck sprang upon Sol-leks in a fury, driving him back and standing in his place.

"Eh? eh?" Francois cried, slapping his thighs gleefully. "Look at dat Buck. Heem keel dat Spitz, heem t'ink to take de job."

"Go 'way!" he cried, but Buck refused to budge.

He took Buck by the scruff of the neck, and though the dog growled threateningly, dragged him to one side and replaced Sol-leks. The old dog did not like it and showed plainly that he was afraid of Buck. Francois was firm, but when he turned his back, Buck again displaced Sol-leks, who was more than willing to go.

Francois was angry. "Now, by Gar, I feex you!" he cried, coming back with a heavy club in his hand.

Buck retreated slowly. He did not attempt to charge in when Sol-leks was brought forward once more. But he circled just beyond the range of the club, snarling with bitterness and rage. While he circled, he watched the club so as to dodge it if it was thrown by Francois, for he was wise in the way of clubs.

The driver went about his work and called to Buck when he was ready to put him in his old place in front of Dave. Buck retreated two or three steps. Francois followed him, and again he retreated. After some time of this,

Francois threw down the club, thinking that Buck feared a thrashing. But Buck was in open revolt. He did not want to escape a clubbing; he wanted to have the leadership. It was his by right. He had earned it, and he would not be content with less.

Perrault jumped in. Between them they ran him about for the better part of an hour. They threw clubs at him. He dodged. They cursed him, and he answered with snarls and kept out of their reach. He did not try to run away, but instead he retreated around and around the camp, making it clear that when his desire was met, he would come in and be good.

Francois scratched his head. Perrault looked at his watch and swore. Time was flying, and they should have been on the trail an hour ago. Francois shook his head and grinned sheepishly at Perrault, who shrugged his shoulders in a sign that they were beaten. Then Francois went up to where Sol-leks stood and called to Buck. Buck laughed, as dogs laugh, yet kept his distance. Francois unfastened Sol-leks's traces and put him back in his old place. The team stood harnessed to the sled in an unbroken line, ready for the trail. There was no place for Buck except at the front. Once more Francois called, and once more Buck laughed and kept away.

"T'row down de club," Perrault commanded.

Francois complied, whereupon Buck trotted in, laughing triumphantly, and swung around into position at the head of the team. His traces were fastened, the sled broken out, and with both men running, they dashed out onto the trail.

As highly as the dog-driver had valued Buck, he found, while the day was still young, that he had undervalued him. Buck proudly took up the duties of leadership: where judgment, quick thinking, and quick acting were required, he showed himself the superior even of Spitz. And Francois had never before seen an equal to Spitz.

But it was in setting the rules and making his mates live up to them that Buck excelled. Dave and Sol-leks did not mind the change in leadership. Their business was to toil mightily in the traces. Billee, the good-natured, could lead for all they cared, so long as he kept order. The rest of the team, however, had grown unruly during the last days of Spitz and were greatly surprised now that Buck proceeded to lick them into shape.

Pike, who pulled at Buck's heels, and who never put an ounce more of his weight against the breast-band than he was forced to, was swiftly and repeatedly shaken for loafing. And after the first day was done, he was pulling more than ever before. The first night in camp, Joe, the sour one, was punished—a thing that Spitz had never succeeded in doing. Buck simply smothered him by virtue of superior weight and cut him up till he ceased snapping and began to whine for mercy.

The general tone of the team picked up immediately. It recovered its old-time solidarity, and once more the dogs leaped as one dog in the traces. Two native huskies were soon added, and the speed with which Buck broke them in took away Francois' breath:

"Nevaire such a dog as dat Buck!" he cried. "No, nevaire! Heem worth one t'ousan' dollair, by Gar! Eh? Wot you say, Perrault?"

And Perrault nodded. He was ahead of the record time then and gaining day by day. The trail was in excellent condition, well packed and hard. It was not too cold. The temperature dropped to fifty below zero and remained there the whole trip. The men rode and ran by turn, and the dogs were kept on the jump, with infrequent stoppages.

The Thirty Mile River was coated with ice, and they covered in one day going out what had taken them ten days coming in. In one run they made a sixty-mile dash from the foot of

Lake Le Barge to the White Horse Rapids. They crossed seventy miles of lakes and flew so fast that the man whose turn it was to run was towed behind the sled at the end of a rope. And by the end of the second week, they topped White Pass and dropped down the sea slope with the lights of Skaguay at their feet.

It was a record run. Each day for fourteen days they had averaged forty miles. For three days Perrault and Francois were deluged with invitations to drink, while the team was the constant center of a worshipful crowd. Next came official orders. Francois called Buck to him, threw his arms around him, and wept over him. And that was the last of Francois and Perrault. Like other men, they passed out of Buck's life for good.

A Scotch half-breed took charge of Buck and his mates, and along with a dozen other dog-teams, he started back over the weary trail to Dawson. It was no light running now, nor record time, but heavy toil each day, with a heavy load behind, for this was the mail train, carrying word from the world to the men who sought gold under the shadow of the Pole.

Buck did not like it, but he bore up well to the work, taking pride in it, and seeing that his mates, whether they took pride in it or not, did their fair share. It was a monotonous life.

One day was like another. At the same time each morning the cooks got up, fires were built, and breakfast was eaten. Then, while some broke camp, others harnessed the dogs, and they were under way an hour or so before dawn. At night, camp was made and the dogs were fed. To them, this was the one feature of the day, though it was good to loaf around for an hour or so with the other dogs, of which there were sixty or more. There were fierce fighters among them, but three battles with the fiercest brought Buck to mastery, so that when he bristled and showed his teeth, they got out of his way.

Best of all, perhaps, he loved to lie near the fire, hind legs crouched under him, forelegs stretched out in front, head raised, and eyes blinking dreamily at the flames. Sometimes he thought of Judge Miller's big house, but more often he remembered the man in the red sweater, the death of Curly, the great fight with Spitz, and the good things he had eaten or would like to eat. He was not homesick. The Sunland was very dim and distant, and such memories had no power over him. Far more potent were the memories of his heredity that made things he had never seen before seem familiar.

It was a hard trip, and the heavy work

wore them down. They were in poor condition when they reached Dawson and should have had a ten days' or a week's rest at least. But in two days' time they left again, loaded with letters for the outside. The dogs were tired, the drivers grumbling, and to make matters worse, it snowed every day. This meant a soft trail and heavier pulling for the dogs. Yet the drivers were fair through it all and did their best for the animals.

Each night the dogs were attended to first. They ate before the drivers ate, and no man prepared to sleep himself till he had examined the feet of the dogs he drove. Still, their strength went down. Since the beginning of the winter they had traveled eighteen hundred miles, dragging sleds the whole weary distance. Buck endured it, keeping his mates up to their work and maintaining discipline, though he, too, was very tired. Billee cried regularly in his sleep each night. Joe was more sour than ever, and Sol-leks was unapproachable, blind side or other side.

But it was Dave who suffered most of all. Something had gone wrong with him. He became more morose and irritable, and when camp was pitched, he immediately made his nest, where his driver fed him. Once out of the harness and down, he did not get on his feet again till harness-up time in the morning. Sometimes, in the traces, when jerked by a sudden stop of the sled, he would cry out with pain. The driver examined him but could find nothing. All the drivers became interested in his case. He was brought from his nest to the fire and was pressed and prodded till he cried out many times. Something was wrong inside, but they could locate no broken bones.

He became so weak that he was falling repeatedly in the traces. The Scotch half-breed called a halt and took him out of the team, moving Sol-leks into his place. His intention was to rest Dave, letting him run free behind the sled. Sick as he was, Dave resented being taken out, grunting and growling while the traces were unfastened, and whimpering broken-heartedly when he saw Sol-leks in the position he had held so long. For the pride of trace and trail was his, and, sick unto death, he could not bear that another dog should do his work.

When the sled started, he floundered in the soft snow alongside the beaten trail, attacking Sol-leks with his teeth, striving to leap inside his traces and get between him and the sled, and all the while whining and yelping and crying with grief and pain. The half-breed tried to drive him away with the whip; but he paid no heed to the stinging lash, and the man did not have the heart to strike harder. Dave refused to run quietly on the trail behind the sled, where the going was easy, but continued to flounder alongside in the soft snow, where the going was most difficult. Then, exhausted, he fell, and lay where he fell, howling mournfully as the long train of sleds churned by.

With the last remnant of his strength, he managed to stagger along behind till the train made another stop, when he floundered past the sleds to his place, where he stood alongside Sol-leks. His driver lingered a moment to get a light for his pipe from the man behind. Then he returned and started his dogs. They swung out on the trail with a remarkable lack of energy and stopped in surprise. The driver was surprised, too. The sled had not moved. He called his comrades to witness the sight. Dave had bitten through both of Sol-leks' traces, and was standing directly in front of the sled in his proper place.

He pleaded with his eyes to remain there. The driver was perplexed. His comrades talked of how a dog could break its heart by being denied the work that killed it. They recalled instances where dogs, too old for the toil or injured, had died because they were cut out of the traces. They decided mercifully, since Dave was to die anyway, that he should die in the traces, heart-easy and content. So he was harnessed in again, and proudly he pulled as of old, though more than once he cried out involuntarily in pain. Several times he fell down and was dragged in the traces, and once the sled ran over him so that he limped thereafter.

But he held out till camp was reached, when his driver made a place for him by the fire. Morning found him too weak to travel. At harness-up time he tried to crawl to his driver. He got on his feet, staggered, and fell. Then he wormed his way forward slowly toward where the harnesses were being put on his mates. He would drag his body forward a few inches at a time until his strength left him. The last his mates saw him, he lay gasping in the snow and yearning toward them. They could hear him mournfully howling till they passed out of sight.

Here the train was halted. The Scotch halfbreed slowly retraced his steps to the camp they had left. The men ceased talking. A revolver shot rang out. The man came back hurriedly. The whips snapped, the bells tinkled merrily, the sleds churned along the trail. But Buck knew, and every dog knew, what had taken place behind the belt of river trees.

CHAPTER 5

The Toil of Trace and Trail

Thirty days from the time they left Dawson, Buck and his mates arrived at Skaguay. They were in a wretched state, worn out and worn down. Buck's one hundred and forty pounds had dwindled to one hundred and fifteen. The rest of his mates had lost even more weight. Pike, who, in his lifetime of deceit, had often faked a hurt leg, was now limping in earnest. Sol-leks too was limping, and Dub was suffering from a wrenched shoulderblade.

Their feet were terribly sore. No spring or rebound was left in them—they were just dead tired. Tiredness that comes from the slow and prolonged draining of strength during months of toil. There was no power of recuperation left, no reserve strength to call upon. It had all been used, every last least bit of it. Every muscle, every fiber, every cell, was tired, dead tired. In less than five months they had traveled twenty-five hundred miles, and during the last eighteen hundred they had only five days' rest. When they arrived at Skaguay, they could barely keep the traces taut, and on the downgrades they just managed to keep out of the way of the sled.

"Mush on, poor sore feets," the driver encouraged them as they tottered down the main street of Skaguay. "Dis is de last. Den we get one long rest. Eh? For sure. One bully long rest."

The drivers themselves confidently expected a long stopover. They had covered twelve hundred miles with just two days' rest and deserved a break. But there were so many men who had rushed into the Klondike, and so many sweethearts, wives, and kin back home, that there were mountains of mail to be delivered. Also, there were official orders. Fresh batches of dogs were to take the places of those dogs now too worn out for the trail.

Three days passed, during which time Buck and his mates realized how really tired and weak they were. Then, on the morning of the fourth day, two men from the States came along and bought them, harness and all, for a song. The men addressed each other as Hal and Charles. Charles was a middle-aged man, with weak and watery eyes and a mustache that twisted fiercely up, concealing a drooping lip. Hal was a youngster of nineteen or twenty, with a big Colt revolver and a hunting knife strapped about him on a belt that bristled with cartridges. This belt was the most noticeable thing about him. Both men were clearly out of place, and why they would venture into the North was a mystery.

Buck heard the bargaining, saw the money pass between the men, and knew that like the mail-train drivers, now the Scotch half-breed was passing out of his life. When driven with his mates to the new owners' camp, Buck saw a slipshod and slovenly affair, tent half stretched, dishes unwashed, everything in disorder. Also, he saw a woman named Mercedes. She was Charles's wife and Hal's sister—a nice family party.

Buck watched them apprehensively as they proceeded to take down the tent and load the sled. The tent was rolled into an awkward bundle three times as large as it should have been. The tin dishes were packed away unwashed.

Mercedes continually fluttered in the way of her men, chattering with advice. When they put a sack of clothes on the front of the sled, she suggested it go on the back; and when they had put it on the back, she discovered over-looked articles which could go nowhere else but in that very sack, and they unloaded it again.

Three men from a neighboring tent came out and looked on, grinning and winking at one another.

"You've got a right smart load as it is," said one of them; "and it's not me should tell you your business, but I wouldn't tote that tent along if I was you."

"However in the world could I manage without a tent?" cried Mercedes, throwing up her hands in dainty dismay.

"It's springtime, and you won't get any more cold weather," the man replied.

She shook her head decidedly, and Charles and Hal put the last odds and ends on top of the mountainous load.

"Think it'll ride?" one of the men asked.

"Why shouldn't it?" Charles demanded rather shortly.

"Oh, that's all right, that's all right," the man hastened meekly to say. "I was just a-won-derin', that is all. It seemed a mite top-heavy."

Charles turned his back and drew the strappings down as well as he could, which was not in the least well.

"An' of course the dogs can hike along all day with that contraption behind them," affirmed a second of the men.

"Certainly," said Hal, with freezing politeness, taking hold of the sled with one hand and swinging his whip from the other. "Mush!" he shouted. "Mush on there!"

The dogs sprang against the breast-bands, strained hard for a few moments, then relaxed. They were unable to move the sled.

"The lazy brutes, I'll show them," he cried, preparing to lash out at them with the whip.

But Mercedes interfered, crying, "Oh, Hal, you mustn't," as she caught hold of the whip and wrenched it from him. "The poor dears! Now you must promise you won't be harsh with them for the rest of the trip, or I won't go a step."

"Precious lot you know about dogs," her brother sneered; "and I wish you'd leave me alone. They're lazy, I tell you, and you've got to whip them to get anything out of them. That's their way. You ask any one. Ask one of those men."

Mercedes looked at them imploringly, distaste at the sight of pain written in her pretty face.

"They're weak as water, if you want to know," came the reply from one of the men. "Plum tuckered out, that's what's the matter. They need a rest."

"Rest be blanked," said Hal, with his beardless lips; and Mercedes said, "Oh!" in pain and sorrow at the oath.

But she was a clannish creature, and rushed at once to the defense of her brother. "Never mind that man," she said pointedly. "You're driving our dogs, and you do what you think best with them."

Again Hal's whip fell upon the dogs. They threw themselves against the breast-bands, dug their feet into the packed snow, and pushed forth with all their strength. The sled held as though it were an anchor. After two efforts, they stood still, panting. The whip was whistling savagely, when once more Mercedes interfered. She dropped on her knees before Buck, with tears in her eyes, and put her arms around his neck.

"You poor, poor dears," she cried sympathetically, "why don't you pull hard?—then you wouldn't be whipped." Buck did not like her, but he was feeling too miserable to resist her, accepting it as part of the day's miserable work.

One of the onlookers, who had been clenching his teeth to suppress hot speech, now spoke up.

"It's not that I care a whoop what becomes of you, but for the dogs' sakes I just want to tell you, you can help them a mighty lot by breaking out that sled. The runners are frozen fast."

A third time the attempt was made, but this time, following the advice, Hal broke out the runners which had been frozen to the snow. The overloaded and unwieldy sled forged ahead with Buck and his mates struggling frantically under the rain of blows. A hundred yards ahead the path turned and sloped steeply into the main street. It would have required an experienced man to keep the top-heavy sled upright, and Hal was not such a man. As they swung on the turn the sled turned over. The dogs never stopped. The lightened sled bounded on its side behind them. They were angry because of the ill treatment and the unjust load. Buck was raging. He broke into a run, the team following his lead. Hal cried "Whoa! whoa!" but they gave no heed. He tripped and was pulled off his feet. The capsized sled ran over him, and the dogs dashed on up the street, adding to the gaiety of Skaguay as they scattered the remainder of the outfit along its chief thoroughfare.

Kind-hearted citizens caught the dogs and gathered up the scattered belongings. Also, they gave advice: Half the load and twice the dogs was what they said. Unwillingly, Hal and Charles listened and overhauled the outfit. Canned goods were unpacked that made men laugh, for canned goods on the trail are a thing to dream about. "Blankets for a hotel" said one of the men who laughed and helped. "Half as many is too much; get rid of them. Throw away that tent, and all those dishes—who's going to wash them, anyway? Good Lord, do you think you're traveling on a train?"

And so it went, getting rid of everything that was not needed. Mercedes cried when her clothes-bags were dumped on the ground and article after article was thrown out. She vowed she would not go an inch. She appealed to everybody and to everything, finally wiping her eyes and proceeding to cast out even articles of apparel that were necessities. And in her zeal, when she had finished with her own, she attacked the belongings of her men and went through them like a tornado.

This accomplished, the outfit, though cut

in half, was still a formidable bulk. Charles and Hal went out in the evening and bought six Outside dogs. These, added to the six of the original team, and the huskies they obtained at the Rink Rapids on the record trip, brought the team up to fourteen. But the Outside dogs did not amount to much. Three were short-haired pointers, one was a Newfoundland, and the other two were mongrels. These newcomers did not seem to know anything. Buck and his comrades looked upon them with disgust, and though he speedily taught them their places and what not to do, he could not teach them what to do. They did not take kindly to trace and trail. With the exception of the two mongrels, they were bewildered and spirit-broken by the ill treatment they had received. The two mongrels were without spirit at all.

With the newcomers hopeless and forlorn, and the old team worn out by twenty-five hundred miles of continuous trail, the outlook was anything but bright. The two men, how-ever, were quite cheerful. And proud, too. They were doing this in style, with fourteen dogs. Never had they seen a sled with as many as fourteen dogs. But there was a reason why fourteen dogs should not drag one sled—that was that one sled could not carry the food for fourteen dogs. But Charles and Hal did not know this. They had worked the trip out on paper, so much to a dog, so many dogs, so many days, Mercedes looked over their shoulders and nodded. It was all so very simple.

Late the next morning Buck led the long team up the street. There was nothing lively about it. They were starting out dead weary. He had made this same trip four times, and the knowledge that, jaded and tired, he was facing the same trail once more made him bitter. His heart was not in the work, nor was the heart of any dog. The Outsiders were timid and frightened; the Insiders had no confidence in their masters.

Buck felt there was no depending upon these two men and the woman. They did not know how to do anything, and as the days went by, it became apparent that they could not learn. They were slack in all things, without order or discipline. It took them half the night to pitch a slovenly camp, and half the morning to break that camp and get the sled loaded so sloppily that they spent the rest of the day stopping and rearranging the load. Some days they did not even travel ten miles. On other days they were unable to get started at all. And they never succeeded in making more than half the distance used by the men as a basis in their dog-food computation.

It was inevitable that they would be short of dog-food. But they hastened it by overfeeding. And when, in addition to this, the worn-out huskies pulled weakly, Hal decided that the planned ration was too small. He doubled it. And to top it all, when Mercedes, with tears in her eyes, could not cajole him into giving the dogs still more, she stole from the fish-sacks and fed them on the sly. But it was not food that Buck and the huskies needed; it was rest. And though they were making poor time, the heavy load they dragged sapped their strength severely.

Then came the underfeeding. Hal awoke one day to the fact that his dog-food was half gone and the distance only a quarter covered. So he cut down the ration and tried to increase the day's travel. It was a simple matter to give the dogs less food, but it was impossible to make the dogs travel faster. And their own inability to get under way earlier in the morning prevented them from traveling longer hours. Not only did they not know how to work the dogs, but they did not know how to work themselves.

The first to go was Dub. Poor blundering thief that he was, he had nonetheless been a faithful worker. His wrenched shoulderblade, untreated and unrested, went from bad to worse, till finally Hal shot him with his revolver.

An Outside dog will starve to death on the ration of the husky, so the six Outside dogs under Buck certainly could not survive on half the ration of the husky. The Newfoundland went first, followed by the three short-haired pointers, the two mongrels hanging more grittily on to life, but going in the end.

By this time, Arctic travel had lost its glamour and became a reality too harsh for these travelers. Mercedes ceased weeping over the dogs, being too occupied with weeping over herself. The one thing they were never too weary to do was to quarrel. They were stiff and in pain; their muscles ached, their bones ached, their very hearts ached. Because of this they became impatient with each other, and harsh words were on their lips first thing in the morning and last at night.

Charles and Hal each believed that he did more than his share of the work, and neither passed up a chance to express this belief. Sometimes Mercedes sided with her husband, sometimes with her brother. The result was an unending family quarrel. They could start with a dispute as to who should chop wood for the fire. Eventually the rest of the family would be dragged into the argument—fathers, mothers, uncles, cousins, people thousands of miles away, some of them dead. They argued about Hal's views on art and Charles's political prejudices. In the meantime the fire remained unbuilt, the camp half pitched, and the dogs unfed.

Mercedes nursed a special grievance. She was pretty and soft and had been treated chivalrously all her days. But the present treatment by her husband and brother was anything but chivalrous. It was her custom to be helpless. She no longer considered the dogs, and because she was sore and tired, she persisted in riding on the sled. She was pretty and soft, but she weighed one hundred and twenty pounds—a lusty last straw to the load dragged by the weak and starving animals. She rode for days, till they fell in the traces and the sled stood still. Charles and Hal begged her to get off and walk.

On one occasion they took her off the sled by brute strength. They never did it again. She let her legs go limp like a spoiled child and sat down on the trail. They went on their way, but she did not move. After they had traveled three miles they unloaded the sled, came back for her, and again by brute strength put her back on the sled.

In their own misery they were callous to the suffering of their animals. Hal's theory was that one must get hardened. He had started out preaching it to his sister and brother-in-law. Failing there, he hammered it into the dogs with a club. At the Five Fingers the dog-food gave out, and a toothless old squaw offered to trade them a few pounds of frozen horsehide for the revolver on Hal's hip. A poor substitute for food, in its frozen state it was more like strips of galvanized iron, and when it reached a dog's stomach it turned into thin leathery string, irritating and indigestible.

And through it all Buck staggered along at the head of the team as in a nightmare. He pulled when he could. When he could no longer pull, he fell down and remained down till blows from the whip or club drove him to his feet again. All the gloss had gone out of his beautiful furry coat. His hair hung down, limp and draggled, or matted with dried blood where Hal's club had bruised him. His muscles had wasted away, and the flesh pads had disappeared, so that each rib and every bone in his frame were outlined cleanly through the loose hide that was wrinkled in folds of emptiness. It was heartbreaking, but Buck's heart was unbreakable. The man in the red sweater had proved that.

As it was with Buck, so was it with his mates. They were moving skeletons. There were seven all together, including him. In their very great misery they had become insensitive to the bite of the whip or the bruise of the club. The pain of the beating was dull and distant. They were barely alive. They were simply bags of bones in which sparks of life faintly fluttered. When the sled halted, they dropped down in the traces like dead dogs, and the spark dimmed and paled and seemed to go out. And when the club or whip fell upon them, the spark fluttered feebly up, and they tottered to their feet and staggered on.

There came a day when Billee, the good-natured, fell and could not rise. Hal had traded off his revolver, so he took the axe and knocked Billee on the head as he lay in the traces, then cut the carcass out of the harness and dragged it to one side. Buck saw, and his mates saw, and they knew that this was very close to happening to them. On the next day Koona went, and but five of them remained: Joe, too far gone to even be mean; Pike, crippled and limping, only half conscious; Sol-leks, the one-eyed, still faithful to the toil of trace and trail, and sorrowful that he had so little strength with which to pull; Teek, who had not traveled so far that winter and who was now beaten more than the others because he was fresher; and Buck, still at the head of the team, but no longer enforcing discipline or striving to enforce it, blind with weakness half the time and keeping to the trail by the dim feel of his feet.

It was beautiful spring weather, but neither dogs nor humans were aware of it. Each day the sun rose earlier and set later. It was dawn by three in the morning, and twilight lingered till nine at night. The whole long day was a blaze of sunshine. The ghostly winter silence had given way to the great spring murmur of awakening life. This murmur arose from all the land, filled with the joy of living. Things which had not moved during the long months of frost came to life and moved again. The sap was rising in the pines. The willows and aspens were bursting out in young buds. Shrubs and vines were putting on fresh garbs of green. Crickets sang in the nights, and in the days, creeping, crawling things rustled forth into the sun. Partridges and woodpeckers were booming and knocking in the forest. Squirrels were chattering, birds singing, and overhead wild fowl honked, driving up from the south in wedges that split the air.

From every hill slope came the trickle of running water, the music of unseen fountains. All things were thawing, bending, snapping. The Yukon was straining to break loose the ice that bound it down. It ate away from beneath; the sun ate from above. Air holes formed, cracks sprang and spread apart, while thin sections of ice fell through into the river. And amid all this bursting and throbbing of awakening life, under the blazing sun and through the soft-sighing breezes, like travelers on their way to death, staggered the two men, the woman, and the huskies.

With the dogs falling, Mercedes weeping and riding, Hal swearing, and Charles's eyes wistfully watering, they staggered into John Thornton's camp at the mouth of White River. When they halted, the dogs dropped down as though they had all been struck dead. Mercedes dried her eyes and looked at John Thornton. Charles, feeling very stiff, very slowly sat down on a log to rest. Hal did the talking. John Thornton was whittling the last touches on an axe-handle he had made from a stick of birch. He whittled and listened, gave one-syllable replies, and, when it was asked, terse advice. He knew the type, and he gave his advice knowing that it would not be followed.

"They told us up above that the bottom was dropping out of the trail and that the best thing for us to do was to lay over," Hal said in response to Thornton's warning to take no more chances on the melting ice. "They told us we couldn't make White River, and here we are." This last remark had a sneering ring of triumph in it.

"And they told you true," John Thornton answered. "The bottom's likely to drop out at any moment. Only fools, with the blind luck of fools, could have made it. I tell you straight, I wouldn't risk my carcass on that ice for all the gold in Alaska."

"That's because you're not a fool, I suppose," said Hal. "All the same, we'll go on to Dawson." He uncoiled his whip. "Get up there, Buck! Hi! Get up there! Mush on!"

Thornton went on whittling. It was idle, he knew, to get between a fool and his folly. He knew that two or three fools more or less would not alter the scheme of things.

But the team did not get up at Hal's command. For quite some time, blows of the whip had been required to rouse the dogs. The whip flashed out, here and there, to no avail. John Thornton compressed his lips. Sol-leks was the first to crawl to his feet. Teek followed. Joe came next, yelping with pain. Pike made painful efforts. Twice he fell over, when half up, and on the third attempt managed to rise. Buck made no effort. He lay quietly where he had fallen. The lash bit into him again and again, but he neither whined nor struggled.

Several times Thornton started, as though to speak, but changed his mind. Moisture came into his eyes, and, as the whipping continued, he arose and walked hesitantly up and down.

This was the first time Buck had failed, and it drove Hal into a rage. He exchanged the whip for the club. Buck refused to move even under the rain of heavier blows that now fell upon him. Like his mates, he was barely able to get up. But, unlike them, he had made up his mind not to get up. He had a vague feeling of impending doom. With the thin and rotten ice he had felt under his feet all day, he sensed disaster close at hand, out there ahead on the ice where his master was trying to drive him. He refused to stir. He had suffered so greatly, and he was so far gone, that the blows did not hurt much. And as they continued to fall upon him, the spark of life within flickered and went down. It was nearly out. He felt strangely numb. As though from a great distance, he was aware that he was being beaten. The last sensations of pain left him. He no longer felt anything, though very faintly he could hear the impact of the club upon his body. But it was no longer his body; it seemed so far away.

And then, suddenly, without warning, uttering a cry that was more like the cry of an animal, John Thornton sprang upon the man who wielded the club. Hal was hurled backward, as though struck by a falling tree. Mercedes screamed. Charles looked on wistfully, wiped his watery eyes, but was so stiff he did not get up.

John Thornton stood over Buck, struggling to control himself, too filled with rage to speak. "If you strike that dog again, I'll kill you," he managed to say in a choking voice.

"It's my dog," Hal replied, wiping the blood from his mouth as he came back. "Get out of my way. I'm going to Dawson."

Thornton stood between him and Buck, with no intention of getting out of the way. Hal drew his long hunting-knife. Mercedes screamed, cried, and laughed, showing signs of hysteria. Thornton rapped Hal's knuckles with the axe-handle, knocking the knife to the ground. He rapped his knuckles again as he tried to pick it up. Then he stooped, picked it up himself, and with two strokes cut Buck's traces.

Hal had no fight left in him. Besides, his arms were full with his sister, and Buck was too near dead to be of further use in hauling the sled. A few minutes later, they pulled out from the bank and down the river. Buck heard them go and raised his head to see. Pike was leading, Sol-leks was at the wheel, and between were

Joe and Teek. They were limping and staggering. Mercedes was riding the loaded sled. Hal was guiding it, and Charles stumbled along in the rear.

As Buck watched them, Thornton knelt beside him and with rough, kindly hands searched for broken bones. By the time his search had disclosed nothing more than many bruises and a state of terrible starvation, the sled was a quarter of a mile away. Dog and man watched it crawling along over the ice. Suddenly, they saw its back end drop down, as into a rut, and the sled, with Hal clinging to it, jerk into the air. Mercedes' scream came to their ears. They saw Charles turn and make one step to run back, and then a whole section of ice give way and dogs and humans disappear. A yawning hole was all that was to be seen. The bottom had dropped out of the trail.

John Thornton and Buck looked at each other.

"You poor devil," said John Thornton, and Buck licked his hand.

CHAPTER 6
For the Love of a Man

When John Thornton froze his feet the previous December, his partners made him comfortable and left him alone to get well, while they went up the river to get out a raft of logs for Dawson. He was still limping slightly at the time he rescued Buck, but with the continued warm weather, even the slight limp left him. And here, lying by the riverbank through the long spring days, watching the running water, listening lazily to the songs of birds and the hum of nature, Buck slowly won back his strength.

After traveling three thousand miles, a rest was due, and Buck waited while his wounds healed, his muscles swelled out, and the flesh came back to cover his bones. For that matter, they were all loafing—Buck, John Thornton, and Skeet and Nig—waiting for the raft to come to carry them down to Dawson. Skeet was a little Irish setter who early on made friends with Buck. Buck, in a dying condition, was unable to resist her advances. As a mother cat washes her kittens, she washed and cleansed Buck's wounds. Regularly, each morning after he had finished his breakfast, she performed her self-appointed task, till he came to look forward to her attention as much as he did Thornton's. Nig, equally friendly, though less demonstrative, was a huge black dog with eyes that laughed and a boundless good nature.

To Buck's surprise, these dogs showed no jealousy toward him. They seemed to share the kindliness of John Thornton. As Buck grew stronger, they enticed him into playing all sorts of ridiculous games. Thornton himself could not resist joining in. So Buck romped through his recovery and into a new existence.

Love—genuine passionate love—was his for the first time. He had never experienced this at Judge Miller's down in the sun-kissed Santa Clara Valley. With the Judge's sons, it had been a working partnership; with the

Judge's grandsons, a sort of guardianship; and with the Judge himself, a stately and dignified friendship. But love that was feverish and burning—that was adoration, that was madness—it had taken John Thornton to arouse.

This man had saved his life; but more than that, he was the ideal master. Other men saw to the welfare of their dogs from a sense of duty. John Thornton saw to the welfare of his dogs as if they were his own children. And he went further. He never forgot a kindly greeting or a cheering word, and to sit down for a long talk with them was as much his delight as theirs. He had a way of taking Buck's head roughly between his hands, and resting his own head upon Buck's, of shaking him back and forth, all the while cursing him with ill names that to Buck were love names. Buck knew no greater joy than that rough embrace and the sound of his whispered words. So great was his ecstasy it seemed that his heart would leap out of his body. He sprang to his feet, his mouth laughing, his eyes dancing, his throat vibrant with unuttered sound. John Thornton would reverently exclaim, "God! You can all but speak!"

Buck had his own special expression of love. He would often seize Thornton's hand in his mouth and close so fiercely that the flesh bore the impression of his teeth for some time afterward. And as Buck understood his words to be love words, so the man understood this faked bite was a caress.

For the most part, however, Buck's love was expressed in adoration. While he went wild with happiness when Thornton touched him or spoke to him, he did not seek these tokens. Unlike Skeet, who would shove her nose under Thornton's hand and nudge and nudge till petted, or Nig, who would stalk up and rest his great head on Thornton's knee, Buck was content to adore at a distance. He would lie by the hour, eager and alert, at Thornton's feet, looking up into his face, dwelling upon it, studying it, following with keenest interest each fleeting expression, every movement or change of feature. Or, he would lie farther away, watching the outlines of the man and the occasional movements of his body. And often, the strength of Buck's gaze would draw John Thornton's head around, and he would return the gaze, without speech, his heart shining out of his eyes as Buck's heart shone out of his.

For a long time after his rescue, Buck did not let Thornton out of his sight. From the moment he left the tent to when he entered it again, Buck would follow at his heels. He was afraid that Thornton would pass out of his life as all the others had. Even at night, in his dreams, he was haunted by this fear. At such times he would shake off sleep and creep through the chill to the flap of the tent, where he would stand and listen to the sound of his master's breathing.

But in spite of this great love he felt for John Thornton, which reflected his soft civilizing influences, the strain of the primitive which the Northland had aroused in him remained alive and active. He was faithful and devoted, yet he retained his wildness and wiliness. He was a thing of the wild, come in from the wild to sit by John Thornton's fire.

His face and body were scarred by the teeth of many dogs, and he fought as fiercely as ever and more shrewdly. Skeet and Nig were too good-natured for quarreling—besides, they belonged to John Thornton. But a strange dog, no matter what the breed, swiftly acknowledged Buck's supremacy or found himself struggling for life with a terrible antagonist. And Buck was merciless. He had learned well the law of club and fang, and he never passed up an advantage or drew back from a foe. He must master or be mastered, and to show mercy was a weakness. Kill or be killed, eat or be eaten, was the law; and this mandate, out of the depths of Time, he obeyed.

Seasons passed as he sat by John Thornton's fire, a broad-breasted dog, white-fanged and long-furred. But beneath the surface were the shades of all manner of dogs—half-wolves and wild wolves, urgent and prompting, savoring the meat he ate, thirsting for the water he drank, scenting the wind, listening to the sounds made by the wild life in the forest, dictating his moods, and directing his actions.

Each day mankind and the claims of mankind slipped farther from him. Deep in the forest a call was sounding, mysteriously thrilling and alluring. He felt compelled to turn his back upon the fire and the earth around it and to plunge into the forest. He knew not where or why. The call sounded deep in the forest and he followed. But his love for John Thornton always drew him back to the fire again.

Thornton alone had this hold on him. The rest of mankind was nothing. Chance travelers might praise or pet him, but he was cold to it all, and he would get up and walk away from too demonstrative a man. When Thornton's partners, Hans and Pete, arrived on the long-expected raft, Buck refused to notice them till he learned they were close to Thornton. After that he tolerated them in a passive sort of way. They were the same large type as Thornton, thinking simply and seeing clearly. They understood Buck and his ways and did not insist upon the intimacy they shared with Skeet and Nig.

For Thornton, however, his love seemed to grow and grow. He, alone among men, could put a pack upon Buck's back for summer traveling. Nothing was too great for Buck to do when Thornton commanded. One day the men and dogs were sitting on the crest of a cliff which fell away, straight down, to naked bedrock three hundred feet below. John Thornton was sitting near the edge, Buck at his shoulder. A thoughtless whim seized Thornton, and he drew the attention of Hans and Pete to the experiment he had in mind. "Jump, Buck!" he commanded, sweeping his arm out and over the chasm. The next instant he was grappling with Buck on the extreme edge, while Hans and Pete were dragging them back to safety.

"It's uncanny," Pete said, after it was over and they had regained their speech.

Thornton shook his head. "No, it is splendid, and it is terrible, too. Do you know, it sometimes makes me afraid."

"I'm not hankering to be the man that lays

hands on you while he's around," Pete announced conclusively, nodding his head toward Buck.

"Py Jingo!" was Hans's contribution. "Not mineself either."

It was at Circle City, before the year was out, that Pete's apprehensions were realized. "Black" Burton, an evil-tempered and malicious man, had been picking a quarrel with a tenderfoot at the bar, when Thornton stepped good-naturedly between them. Buck, as was his custom, was lying in a corner, head on paws, watching his master's every action. Burton struck out, without warning, straight from the shoulder. Thornton was sent spinning, saving himself from falling only by clutching the rail of the bar.

Those who were watching heard what was best described as a roar, and they saw Buck's body rise up in the air as he left the floor and went for Burton's throat. The man saved his life by instinctively throwing out his arm but was hurled backward to the floor with Buck on top of him. Buck loosed his teeth from the flesh of his arm and drove in again for the throat. This time the man succeeded only in partly blocking the attack and his throat was torn open. Then the crowd was upon Buck, and he was driven off. But while a surgeon checked the bleeding, he prowled up and down, growling furiously, attempting to rush in, and being forced back by an array of hostile clubs. A "miners' meeting," called on the spot, decided that the dog had sufficient provocation, and Buck was discharged. But his reputation was made, and from that day his name spread through every camp in Alaska.

Later on, in the fall of the year, he saved John Thornton's life in quite another fashion. The three partners were steering a long and narrow poling-boat down a bad stretch of rapids. Hans and Pete moved along the bank, guiding it from tree to tree with a thin manila rope, while Thornton remained in the boat, directing its descent by means of a pole, and shouting directions to the shore. Buck, on the bank, worried and anxious, kept abreast of the boat, his eyes never off his master.

At a particularly bad spot, where a ledge of barely submerged rocks jutted out into the river, Hans cast off the rope, while Thornton poled the boat out into the stream to guide it when it had cleared the ledge. It was flying downstream in a swift current when Hans checked it with the rope too suddenly. The boat turned over, and Thornton, flung sheer out of it, was carried downstream toward the worst part of the rapids, a stretch of wild water in which no swimmer could survive.

Buck sprang in instantly, and at the end of three hundred yards, amid a mad swirl of water, he reached Thornton. When he felt him grasp his tail, Buck headed for the bank, swimming with all his splendid strength. But the progress shoreward was slow, the progress downstream amazingly rapid. From below came the fatal roaring of the wild current. The pull of the water as it took the beginning of the last steep pitch was frightful, and Thornton knew that reaching shore was impossible. He scraped furiously against one rock, bruised across a second, and struck a third with crushing force. He clutched its slippery top with both hands, releasing Buck, and above the roar of the churning water shouted: "Go, Buck! Go!"

Buck could not hold his own and was swept on downstream, struggling desperately. When he heard Thornton's command repeated, he partly reared out of the water, throwing his head high, as though for a last look, then turned obediently toward the bank. He swam powerfully and was dragged ashore by Pete and Hans at the very point where swimming ceased to be possible.

They knew it was only for a matter of minutes that a man could cling to a slippery rock in the face of that driving current, and they ran as fast as they could up the bank to a point far above where Thornton was hanging on. They attached the line with which they had been steering the boat to Buck's neck and shoulders, being careful that it should neither strangle him nor impede his swimming, and launched him into the stream. He struck out boldly but not straight enough into the stream. He discovered the mistake too late. Thornton was just a half-dozen strokes away ,and Buck was being carried helplessly past.

Hans promptly pulled back the rope as though Buck were a boat. The rope tightened on him in the sweep of the current, and he was jerked under the surface, where he remained till his body struck against the bank and he was hauled out. He was half drowned, and Hans and Pete threw themselves upon him, pounding breath into him and the water out of him. He staggered to his feet and fell down. The faint sound of Thornton's voice came to them, and though they could not make out the words, they knew that he called with desperation. His master's voice acted on Buck like an electric shock. He sprang to his feet and ran up the bank again.

Again the rope was attached and he was launched, but this time he leaped straight into the stream. He had miscalculated once, but this would not happen a second time. Hans let out the rope, permitting no slack, while Pete kept it free of coils. Buck held on till he was on a line straight above Thornton; then he turned, and with the speed of an express train headed down upon him. Thornton saw him coming, and as Buck struck him like a battering ram, with the whole force of the current behind him, he reached up and wrapped both his arms around the shaggy neck. Hans pulled the rope, and Buck and Thornton were jerked under the water. Strangling, suffocating, sometimes one uppermost and sometimes the other, dragging over the jagged bottom, smashing against rocks and snags, they veered into the bank.

When Thornton regained consciousness, his first glance was for Buck, over whose limp and apparently lifeless body Nig was howling, while Skeet was licking his wet face and closed eyes. Thornton, himself bruised and battered, went carefully over Buck's body, when he had been revived, finding three broken ribs.

"That settles it," he announced. "We camp right here." And camp they did, till Buck's ribs healed and he was able to travel.

That winter at Dawson, Buck performed another feat, not so heroic, perhaps, but one that put his name many notches higher on the totem pole of Alaskan fame. This feat was particularly gratifying to the three men, for they were in need of the outfit which it furnished, and it enabled them to make a long-desired trip into the virgin East, where miners had not yet appeared. It was brought about by a conversation in the Eldorado Saloon, in which men boasted about their favorite dogs. Buck, because of his record, was the target for these men, and Thornton was driven stoutly to defend him. One man stated that his dog could start a sled with five hundred pounds and walk off with it; a second bragged six hundred for his dog; and a third, seven hundred.

"Pooh! Pooh!" said John Thornton; "Buck can start a thousand pounds."

"And break it out? And walk off with it for a hundred yards?" demanded Matthewson.

"And break it out, and walk off with it for a hundred yards," John Thornton said coolly.

"Well," Matthewson said, slowly and deliberately, so that all could hear, "I've got a thousand dollars that says he can't. And there it is." So saying, he slammed a sack of gold dust the size of a bologna sausage down upon the bar.

Nobody spoke. Thornton's bluff, if bluff it was, had been called. He could feel a flush of warm blood creeping up his face. His tongue had tricked him. He did not know whether Buck could start a thousand pounds. Half a ton! The enormousness of it appalled him. He had great faith in Buck's strength and had often thought him capable of starting such a load; but he had never faced the reality of it. The eyes of a dozen men fixed upon him, silent and waiting. And further, he did not have a thousand dollars.

"I've got a sled standing outside now, with twenty fifty-pound sacks of flour on it," Matthewson went on with brutal directness; "so don't let that stop you."

Thornton did not reply. He did not know what to say. He glanced from face to face in the way of a man who has lost the power of thought. The face of Jim O'Brien, an old-time comrade, caught his eyes. It was a cue to him, seeming to rouse him to do what he would never have dreamed of doing.

"Can you lend me a thousand?" he asked, almost in a whisper.

"Sure," answered O'Brien, thumping down a sack by the side of Matthewson's. "Though it's little faith I'm having, John, that the beast can do the trick."

The Eldorado emptied its occupants into the street to see the test. The tables were deserted, and the dealers and gamekeepers came out to see the outcome of the wager and to lay odds. Several hundred men, furred and mittened, stood around the sled within easy distance. Matthewson's sled, loaded with a thousand pounds of flour, had been standing for a couple of hours, and in the intense cold (it was sixty below zero) the runners had frozen fast to the hard-packed snow. Men offered odds of two to one that Buck could not budge the sled.

A quibble arose concerning the phrase "break out." O'Brien contended it was Thornton's privilege to knock the runners loose, leaving Buck to "break it out" from a dead standstill. Matthewson insisted that the phrase included breaking the runners from the frozen grip of the snow. A majority of the men who had witnessed the making of the bet decided in Matthewson's favor, and the odds went up to three to one against Buck.

There were no takers. Not a single man believed him capable of this feat. Thornton had been hurried into the wager, heavy with doubt. And now that he looked at the sled itself, with the regular team of ten dogs curled up in the snow before it, the more impossible the task appeared. Matthewson was jubilant.

"Three to one!" he proclaimed. "I'll lay

you another thousand at that figure,
Thornton. What d'ye say?"

Thornton's doubt was strong in his face,
but his fighting spirit was aroused—the fighting spirit that soars above odds and fails to rec-
ognize the impossible. He called to Hans and
Pete. The three partners could pull together
only two hundred dollars. This sum was their
total capital; yet they laid it down without hes-
itation against Matthewson's six hundred.

The team of ten dogs was unhitched, and
Buck, with his own harness, was put onto the
sled. He had caught the excitement, and he
felt that in some way he must do a great thing
for John Thornton. Murmurs of admiration
went up at his splendid appearance. He was in
perfect condition, without an ounce of super-
fluous flesh, and the one hundred and fifty
pounds that he weighed were pounds of grit
and virility. His furry coat shone with the
sheen of silk. Down the neck and across the
shoulders, his mane half bristled and seemed
to lift with every movement. His great chest
and heavy forelegs were in proportion to the
rest of the body, where the muscles showed in
tight rolls underneath the skin. Men felt these
muscles and proclaimed them hard as iron,
and the odds went down to two to one.

"Gad, sir! Gad, sir!" stuttered a member of

the crowd. "I offer you eight hundred for him, sir, before the test, sir; eight hundred just as he stands."

Thornton shook his head and stepped to Buck's side.

"You must stand off from him," Matthewson protested. "Free play and plenty of room."

The crowd fell silent. Everybody acknowledged that Buck was a magnificent animal, but twenty fifty-pound sacks of flour bulked too large in their eyes for them to loosen their pouch-strings.

Thornton knelt down by Buck's side. He took his head in his two hands and rested cheek on cheek. He did not playfully shake him, or murmur soft love curses; but he whispered in his ear. "As you love me, Buck. As you love me." Buck whined with suppressed eagerness.

The crowd was watching curiously. The affair was growing mysterious. As Thornton got to his feet, Buck seized his mittened hand between his jaws, pressing in with his teeth and releasing slowly, half-reluctantly. It was the answer, in terms, not of speech, but of love. Thornton stepped well back.

"Now, Buck," he said.

Buck tightened the traces, then slacked

them for a matter of several inches. It was the way he had learned.

"Gee!" Thornton's voice rang out, sharp in the tense silence.

Buck swung to the right, ending the movement in a plunge that took up the slack and with a sudden jerk arrested his one hundred and fifty pounds. The load quivered, and from under the runners arose a crisp crackling.

"Haw!" Thornton commanded.

Buck duplicated the maneuver, this time to the left. The crackling turned into a snapping, the sled pivoting and the runners slipping and grating several inches to the side. The sled was broken out. Men were holding their breaths.

"Now, MUSH!"

Thornton's command cracked out like a pistol-shot. Buck threw himself forward, tightening the traces with a jarring lunge. His whole body was gathered compactly together in this tremendous effort, the muscles writhing and knotting under the silky fur. His great chest was low to the ground, his head forward and down, while his feet were flying like mad, the claws scarring the hard-packed snow in parallel grooves. The sled swayed and trembled, half-started forward. One of his feet slipped, and one man groaned aloud. Then the sled lurched ahead in what appeared a rapid succession of jerks, though it never really came to a dead stop again . . . half an inch . . . an inch . . . two inches . . . The jerks perceptibly diminished as the sled gained momentum and it was moving steadily along.

Men gasped and began to breathe again, unaware that for a moment they had ceased to breathe. Thornton was running behind, encouraging Buck with short, cheery words. The distance had been measured off, and as he neared the pile of firewood which marked the end of the hundred yards, a cheer began to grow and grow, which burst into a roar as he passed the firewood and halted at command. Every man was cheering, even Matthewson. Hats and mittens were flying in the air. Men were shaking hands, it did not matter with whom, and bubbling over in a general incoherent babble.

But Thornton fell on his knees beside Buck. Head was against head, and he was shaking him back and forth. Those who rushed up heard him talking to Buck, praising him long and fervently, and softly and lovingly.

"Gad, sir! Gad, sir!" came another offer. "I'll give you a thousand for him, sir, a thousand, sir—twelve hundred, sir."

Thornton rose to his feet. His eyes were wet. The tears were streaming freely down his cheeks. "Sir," he said, "no, sir. You can go to hell, sir. It's the best I can do for you, sir."

Buck seized Thornton's hand in his teeth. Thornton shook him back and forth. As though animated by a common impulse, the onlookers drew back to a respectful distance and were discreet enough not to interrupt.

CHAPTER 7

The Sounding of the Call

When Buck earned John Thornton sixteen hundred dollars in five minutes, he made it possible for his master to pay off some debts and to journey with his partners into the East in search of a fabled lost mine. Many men had sought after it; few had found it. More than a few had never returned from the quest. This lost mine was steeped in tragedy and shrouded in mystery. Its site was marked by an ancient and ramshackle cabin. Dying men who swore this mine existed proved it by showing gold nuggets unlike any found in the Northland.

But no man still alive had witnessed this treasure. Now John Thornton and Pete and Hans, with Buck and half a dozen other dogs, took off into the East on an unknown trail to succeed where others had failed.

John Thornton asked little of man or nature. He was unafraid of the wild. With a handful of salt and a rifle, he could plunge into the wilderness wherever he pleased and for as long as he pleased. Being in no rush, he hunted his dinner in the course of the day's travel. If he failed to find it, he kept on traveling, secure in the knowledge that sooner or later he would come to it. So, on this great journey into the East, straight meat was the bill of fare, ammunition and tools principally made up the load on the sled, and time did not matter.

To Buck it was boundless delight—hunting, fishing, and indefinite wandering through strange places. For weeks at a time, they would travel on steadily, day after day. Week after week they would camp here and there, the dogs loafing and the men washing countless pans of dirt by the fire, looking for gold. Sometimes they went hungry; sometimes they feasted riotously, depending on to the abundance of game and the fortune of hunting.

The months came and went, and they twisted back and forth through the uncharted vastness, where now no men could be found, yet where men had been before. They traveled on and on through summer into fall.

And through another winter they wandered on the trails of men who had gone before. Once, they came upon an ancient path blazed through the forest, and the Lost Cabin seemed very near. But the path led nowhere.

Spring came once more, and at the end of their wandering they found, not the Lost Cabin, but a shallow place in a broad valley where the gold shone like yellow butter across the bottom of the washing-pan. They traveled no farther. Each day that they worked earned them thousands of dollars in clean dust and nuggets, and they worked every day. The gold was sacked in moose-hide bags, fifty pounds to the bag, and piled like firewood outside the lodge. Day after day they toiled, as they piled their treasure high.

There was nothing for the dogs to do, except now and again haul in the meat that Thornton killed. Buck spent long hours musing by the fire, seeing images from a time he seemed to know from a life before. And beyond these images, there was the call, sounding in the depths of the forest. It filled him with great unrest and strange desires. It awoke in him wild yearnings for something as yet unknown. Sometimes he pursued the call into the forest, looking for it as though it were a tangible thing, barking softly or defiantly, as the mood might dictate.

Irresistible impulses seized him. He would be lying in camp, dozing lazily in the heat of the day, when suddenly his head would lift and his ears cock, intent and listening. He would spring to his feet and dash away, on and on, for hours, through the forest and across the open spaces. For a day at a time, he would lie in the underbrush watching the wild birds strutting up and down. But especially he loved to run in the dim twilight of the summer nights, listening to the subdued and sleepy murmurs of the forest, and seeking that mysterious something that called to him—called, waking or sleeping, at all times, for him to come.

One night he sprang from sleep with a start, eager-eyed, nostrils quivering, mane bristling. From the forest came the call, distinct and definite as never before—a long-drawn howl, like, yet unlike, any noise made by a husky dog. And he knew it as a sound he had heard before. He sprang through the sleeping camp and in swift silence dashed through the woods. As he drew closer to the cry, he went more slowly, with caution in every movement, till he came to an open place among the trees. And looking out, he saw a long, lean, timber wolf, erect on its haunches, with nose pointed to the sky.

Buck had made no noise, yet it sensed his presence and ceased its howling. Buck stalked into the open, half crouching, body gathered compactly together, tail straight and stiff, feet falling with great care. Every movement combined caution with an overture of friendliness. But the wolf fled at the sight of him. Buck followed leaping wildly, in a frenzy to overtake him. He had him cornered. The wolf whirled about, pivoting on his hind legs like a cornered husky, snarling, bristling, and snapping his teeth.

Buck did not attack, but circled about him and hedged him in with friendly advances. The wolf was suspicious and afraid, for Buck was much heavier and larger. Waiting for his chance, he darted away, and the chase was resumed. Time and again he was cornered, and the chase was repeated.

But in the end, Buck's persistence was rewarded. The wolf, finding that no harm was intended, finally sniffed noses with him. Then they became friendly and played about nervously. After some time the wolf trotted off at an easy lope in a manner that plainly showed he was going somewhere. He made it clear to Buck that he was to come along, and they ran side by side through the twilight, straight up the creek bed, and across the bleak divide.

They came down into level country where there were great stretches of forest and many streams. They ran steadily, hour after hour, the sun rising higher and the day growing warmer. Buck was wildly glad. He knew he was at last answering the call, running by the side of his wild brother toward the place from where the call surely came. Old memories were coming upon him fast. He knew he had done this before, somewhere in that other and dimly remembered world, and he was doing it again, now, running free in the open, the unpacked earth underfoot, the wide sky overhead.

They stopped by a running stream to drink, and stopping, Buck remembered John Thornton. He sat down. The wolf started on toward the place from where the call surely came, then returned to him, sniffing noses and making actions as though to encourage him. But Buck turned about and started slowly to backtrack. For the better part of an hour, his wild brother ran by his side, whining softly. Then he sat down, pointed his nose upward, and howled. It was a mournful howl, and as Buck traveled steadily on his way, he heard it grow faint and fainter until it was lost in the distance.

John Thornton was eating dinner when Buck dashed into camp and sprang upon him in a frenzy of affection, overturning him, scrambling upon him, licking his face, biting his hand, while Thornton shook Buck back and forth and spoke to him lovingly.

For two days and nights Buck never left camp—never let Thornton out of his sight. He followed him about at his work, watched him while he ate, saw him into his blankets at night and out of them in the morning. But after two days, the call in the forest began to sound more strongly than ever. Buck's restlessness came back to him, and he was haunted by recollections of his wild brother, of the land beyond the divide and the run side by side through the wide forest stretches. Once again he took to wandering in the woods, but the wild brother did not come and the mournful howl was never raised.

He began to sleep out at night, staying away from camp for days at a time. Once he crossed the divide and wandered there for a week, seeking vainly for a fresh sign of his wild brother. He killed his meat as he traveled. and traveled with a long, easy lope that seemed never to tire. He fished for salmon in a broad stream that emptied into the sea, and by this stream he killed a large black bear. It was a hard fight, and it aroused the last buried remnants of Buck's fierceness.

The longing for blood became stronger than ever before. He was a killer, a thing that preyed. He lived on other things that lived, unaided and alone. By virtue of his own strength and experience, he survived triumphantly in a hostile environment where only the strong survived. Because of all this, he possessed great pride in himself. His pride advertised itself in all his movements; was apparent in the play of every muscle, in the way he carried himself; and made his glorious furry coat even more glorious. Except for the stray brown on his muzzle and above his eyes, and the splash of white hair that ran down his chest, he might well have been mistaken for a gigantic wolf, larger than the largest of the breed.

His cunning was the cunning of a wolf—wild cunning; his intelligence, the combined intelligence of a shepherd and a St. Bernard. All this, plus experience gained in the fiercest of schools, made him as fearsome a creature as any that roamed the wild. A meat-eating animal living on a straight meat diet, he was at the high tide of his life, overflowing with vigor. Every part, brain and body, nerve tissue and fiber, was keyed to the most exquisite pitch. He responded with lightning-like speed to sights and sounds and events that required action. As quickly as a husky could leap, he could leap twice as quickly. His muscles were charged with vitality and snapped into play sharply, like steel springs. Life streamed through him in splendid flood, until it seemed that it would burst him apart in sheer ecstasy.

"Never was there such a dog," said John Thornton one day, as the partners watched Buck marching out of camp.

"When he was made, the mould was broke," said Pete.

"Py jingo! I t'ink so mineself," Hans affirmed.

They saw him marching out of camp, but they did not see the instant and terrible transformation that took place as soon as he was within the secrecy of the forest. He no longer marched. At once he became a thing of the wild, stealing along softly, cat-footed among the shadows. He knew how to take advantage of every cover, to crawl on his belly like a snake, and to leap and strike. He could take a bird from its nest and kill a rabbit as it slept. Fish, in open pools, were not too quick for him; nor were beaver, mending their dams, too wary. He killed to eat, not from evilness. It was his delight to sneak up on the squirrels, and, when he all but had them, to let them go, chattering in mortal fear to the treetops.

As the fall came on, the moose appeared in greater abundance, moving slowly down into the valleys. Buck had already dragged down a stray young calf, but he longed for larger and more challenging prey. He came upon it one day when a band of twenty moose crossed over from the land of streams and timber, and chief among them was a great bull. He was in a savage temper, and, standing over six feet from the ground, was as alarming a rival as Buck could desire. At the sight of Buck, the bull roared with fury, tossing his great antlers, branching to fourteen points and spanning seven feet from tip to tip. His small eyes burned with a vicious and bitter light.

A feathered arrow protruded from the bull's side, which accounted for his savageness. Guided by his animal instincts, Buck proceeded to separate the bull from the herd. It was no slight task. He would bark and dance about in front of him, just out of reach of the great antlers and strong hoofs that could have stamped his life out with a single blow. Unable to turn his back on the fanged danger and go on, the bull was driven into a rage. At such moments, he charged Buck, who retreated craftily, luring him on. But when he was separated from the herd, two or three of the younger bulls would charge back upon Buck and enable the wounded bull to rejoin the herd.

There is a patience of the wild—a dogged, tireless persistence that holds the spider in his its web, the snake in its coils—holds them motionless for endless hours. This patience is evident in an animal when it hunts its living food. And it belonged to Buck as he stayed with the herd, slowing its march, irritating the young bulls, worrying the cows, and driving the wounded bull mad with helpless rage. This continued for half a day. Buck attacked the herd from all sides, separating his victim as fast as it could rejoin its mates.

As the day wore on, the young bulls retraced their steps, more and more reluctant to come to the aid of their troubled leader. The oncoming winter was forcing them to move to lower levels, but it seemed they could never shake off this tireless creature that held them back. Besides, it was not the life of the herd or of the young bulls being threatened.

As twilight fell, the old bull stood with lowered head, watching his mates—the cows he had known, the calves he had fathered, the bulls he had mastered—as they ambled on at a rapid pace through the fading light. He could not follow, for before him leaped the merciless fanged terror that would not let him go. He weighed more than half a ton. He had lived a long, strong life, full of fight and struggle, and at the end he faced death at the teeth of a creature whose head did not reach beyond his great knuckled knees.

From then on, night and day, Buck never left his prey, never gave it a moment's rest, never permitted it to browse the leaves of trees. Nor did he give the wounded bull opportunity to quench his burning thirst in the slender trickling streams they crossed. Often, in desperation, he burst into long stretches of flight. At such times Buck did not attempt to stop him, but loped easily at his heels, satisfied with the way the game was played, lying down when the moose stood still, attacking him fiercely when he tried to eat or drink.

The great head drooped more and more under its tree of horns, and its awkward trot grew weaker and weaker. He took to standing for long periods, with nose to the ground and dejected ears dropped limply; so Buck found more time in which to get water for himself and to rest. At such moments, with eyes fixed upon the big bull, Buck sensed that a change was coming. He could feel a new stir in the land. Just as the moose were coming into the land, other kinds of life were also appearing. Forest and stream and air seemed to be pulsating with their presence. The awareness of this new life came upon him, not by sight or sound or smell, but by some other and subtler sense. He heard nothing and saw nothing, yet he knew that the land was somehow different, that strange things were afoot. He resolved to investigate after he had finished the business at hand.

At last, at the end of the fourth day, he pulled the great moose down. For a day and a night he remained by the kill, eating and sleeping. Then, rested, refreshed, and strong, he turned his face toward camp and John Thornton. He broke into the long easy lope, and went on, hour after hour, never losing the way, heading straight home through the strange country with a certainness of direction that put man and his compass to shame.

As he traveled steadily on, he became more and more conscious of the new stir in the land. No longer was this a fact he knew in some subtle, mysterious way. The birds talked of it; the squirrels chattered about it; the very breeze whispered of it. Several times he stopped and drew in the fresh morning air in great sniffs, sensing a something that made him leap on with greater speed. He was oppressed with a sense of disaster happening, if it had not already happened. As he crossed the last watershed and dropped down into the valley toward camp, he proceeded with greater caution.

Three miles away he came upon a fresh trail that sent his neck hair bristling. It led straight toward camp and John Thornton. Buck hurried on, swiftly and silently, every nerve straining and tense, alert to the many details which told the story—all but the end. His nose gave him a varying description of the passage of the life on the heels of which he was traveling. He remarked upon the silence of the forest. The bird life had flitted away. The squirrels were in hiding. He saw only one—a sleek gray fellow, dead and flattened against a gray dead limb so that he seemed a part of the wood itself.

As Buck slid along like a gliding shadow, his nose was jerked suddenly to the side as though a force had gripped and pulled it. He followed the new scent into a thicket and found Nig. He was lying on his side, dead where he had dragged himself, an arrow protruding, head and feathers, from either side of his body.

A hundred yards farther on, Buck came upon one of the sled dogs Thornton had bought in Dawson. This dog was thrashing about in a struggle with death, directly on the trail, and Buck walked around him without stopping. From the camp came the faint sound of many voices, rising and falling in a singsong chant. Bellying forward to the edge of the clearing, he found Hans, lying on his face, feathered with arrows like a porcupine. At the same instant Buck peered out where the lodge had been and saw something that made his hair leap straight up on his neck and shoulders. A gust of overpowering rage swept over him. He did not know that he growled, but he growled aloud with a terrible rage. For the last time in his life, he allowed passion to overtake cunning and reason. It was because of his great love for John Thornton that he lost his head.

The Yeehat Indians were dancing about the wreckage of the lodge when they heard a fearful roaring and saw rushing upon them an animal the like of which they had never seen before. It was Buck, a live hurricane of fury, hurling himself upon them in a frenzy to destroy. He sprang at the foremost man (it was the chief), ripping his throat wide open until the jugular spouted a fountain of blood. He did not pause, but with the next bound tore the throat of a second man wide open. There was no resisting him. He plunged about in their very midst, tearing and destroying, in constant and terrific motion, which defied the arrows they shot at him. In fact, his movements were so rapid, and the Indians were so closely tangled together, that they shot one another with the arrows. One young hunter, hurling a spear at Buck in mid-air, drove it through the chest of another hunter with such force that the point broke through the skin of the back and came out the other side. Then a panic seized the Yeehats, and they fled in terror into the woods, proclaiming as they fled the arrival of the Evil Spirit.

And truly Buck was a demon come to life, raging at their heels and dragging them down like deer as they raced through the trees. It was a fateful day for the Yeehats. They scattered far and wide over the country, and it was not till a week later that the last of the survivors gathered together in a lower valley and counted their losses. As for Buck, wearying of the pursuit, he returned to the desolated camp. He found Pete where he had been killed in his blankets in the first moment of surprise. Thornton's desperate struggle was fresh-written on the earth, and Buck sniffed out every detail of it down to the edge of a deep pool. By the edge, head and fore feet in the water, lay Skeet, faithful to the last. The pool itself, muddy and discolored, effectively hid what it contained. And it contained John Thornton—for Buck followed his trace into the water, from which no trace led away.

All day Buck brooded by the pool or roamed restlessly about the camp. He knew death as an ending of movement, as a passing away from the lives of the living. And he knew John Thornton was dead. It left a great void in him, somewhat like hunger, but a void which ached and ached, and which food could not fill. At times, when he paused to contemplate the bodies of the Yeehats, he forgot the pain; and at such times he was aware of a great pride in himself—a pride greater than any he had yet experienced. He had killed man, the noblest game of all. He sniffed the bodies curiously. They had died so easily. It was harder to kill a husky dog than these men. They were no match at all, were it not for their arrows and spears and clubs. From now on, he would be unafraid of them except when they held their arrows, spears, and clubs.

Night came, and a full moon rose high over the trees into the sky, lighting the land till it was bathed in ghostly day. And with the coming of the night, brooding and mourning by the pool, Buck became aware of a stirring of the new life in the forest. He stood up, listening and scenting. From far away drifted a faint, sharp yelp, followed by a chorus of similar sharp yelps. As the moments passed, the yelps grew closer and louder. Again Buck knew them as sounds heard in that other world which persisted in his memory. He walked to the center of the open space and listened. It was the call, the many-noted call, sounding more alluring and compelling than ever before. And as never before, he was ready to obey. John Thornton was dead. The last tie was broken. Man and the claims of man no longer bound him.

Hunting their living meat, the wolf pack had at last crossed over from the land of streams and timber and invaded Buck's valley. Into the clearing where the moonlight streamed, they poured in a silvery flood. In the center of the clearing stood Buck, motionless as a statue, awaiting their arrival. They were in awe, so still and large he stood. They paused a moment's pause, till the boldest one leaped straight for him. Like a flash Buck struck, breaking its neck. Then he stood, without movement, as before, the stricken wolf rolling in agony behind him. Three others tried it in quick succession, and one after the other they drew back, with blood streaming from their slashed throats or shoulders.

This was sufficient to fling the whole pack forward, crowded together, blocked and confused. Buck's marvelous quickness and agility stood him in good stead. Pivoting on his hind legs, and snapping and gashing, he was everywhere at once, whirling swiftly from side to side. But to prevent them from getting behind him, he was forced back, till he came up against a high gravel bank. He ended up with his back to the bank, protected on three sides and with nothing to do but face the front.

And he faced it so well that at the end of half an hour, the wolves drew back perplexed. Their tongues were hanging out, their fangs showing cruelly white in the moonlight. Some were lying down with heads raised and ears pricked forward; others stood on their feet, watching him; and still others were lapping water from the pool. One wolf, long and lean and gray, advanced cautiously, in a friendly manner, and Buck recognized the wild brother with whom he had run for a night and a day. He was whining softly, and, as Buck whined, they touched noses.

Then an old wolf, gaunt and battle-scarred, came forward. Buck twisted his lips into the beginning of a snarl, but sniffed noses with him, whereupon the old wolf sat down, pointed his nose at the moon, and broke out into the long wolf howl. The others sat down and howled. And now the call came to Buck unmistakably. He, too, sat down and howled.

This over, he came out of his corner and the pack crowded around him, sniffing in half-friendly, half-savage manner. The leaders sprang away into the woods. The wolves swung in behind, yelping in chorus. And Buck ran with them, side by side with the wild brother, yelping as he ran.

◆ ◆ ◆

And here may well end the story of Buck. Not many years later, the Yeehats noted a change in the breed of timber wolves—some were seen with splashes of brown on head and muzzle, and with a strip of white down the center of the chest. But more remarkable than this, the Yeehats tell of a Ghost Dog that runs at the head of the pack. They are afraid of this Ghost Dog, for it has great cunning, stealing from their camps in fierce winters, robbing their traps, slaying their dogs, and defying their bravest hunters.

And the tale grows worse. There are hunters who failed to return to their camp, and there have been hunters whose tribesmen were found with throats slashed cruelly open and with wolf prints about them in the snow greater than the prints of any wolf. Each fall, when the Yeehats follow the movement of the moose, there is a certain valley into which they never enter. And the word goes out over the fire of how the Evil Spirit came to select that valley for a place to live.

In the summers there is one visitor to that valley, however. It is a great, gloriously coated wolf, like, and yet unlike, all other wolves. He crosses alone from the great timberland and comes down into an open space among the trees. Here a yellow stream of gold dust flows from rotted moose-hide sacks and sinks into the ground. Long grasses grow through it and mold overruns it and hides its yellow from the sun. Here he muses for a time, howling once, long and mournfully, before he departs.

But he is not always alone. When the long winter nights come on, he may be seen running at the head of the pack through the pale moonlight, leaping gigantic above his mates, his great throat bellowing as he sings the song of the pack.

AFTERWORD
Jonathan Kelley

About Jack London and His Time

The man we know as Jack London was born in San Francisco on January 12, 1876. Nothing about his early days suggested a bright future. His mother, Flora Wellman, named him John Griffith Chaney and said his father was William Chaney, a traveling astrologer. Chaney denied he was the baby's father and deserted Flora. Jack got his last name from his mother's marriage in September, 1876 to a partly disabled Civil War veteran, John London.

Jack's parents were not well-off, and they both had to work hard to pay the bills. Most of Jack's childcare came from Virginia Prentiss, a former slave. Jack called Ms. Prentiss "Aunt Jenny," and she was a good friend to him all his short life.

As a young boy, Jack discovered the love of reading that would start him on the path to becoming a great writer. When he was ten, he began visiting the Oakland Public Library, where a kind librarian encouraged him to read a variety of classic and popular books. Within the covers of those books, he found an exciting world of places and ideas. That discovery thrilled him; he realized that no matter where he was or what he had to do to get by, his mind could never be imprisoned.

As the London family struggled for survival, Jack was expected to do his part, even as a child. He went to work as a paperboy when he was eleven. After finishing eighth grade, he took a job in a cannery. Without child labor laws to protect him, he sometimes worked for eighteen hours a day.

Then, when he was just fifteen, he borrowed three hundred dollars from Aunt Jenny Prentiss and bought a little boat, which he named the *Razzle Dazzle*. This boat was no rich boy's plaything. With it, Jack embarked on a career as an "oyster pirate"—a sailor who illegally helped himself to oysters growing in private beds in the San Francisco Bay. Jack was a daring young man, and he soon earned himself the title of "Prince of the Oyster Pirates."

But while Jack loved this adventurous life, he was no fool. Looking around him, he realized that an oyster pirate's career was short. Most pirates ended up either dead or in jail. So he hit upon an ingenious idea: in order to keep on sailing and living a life of risk and adventure, he would simply jump over to the other side of the law. He became a deputy patrolman with the California Fish Patrol. His job? Chasing down and arresting oyster pirates.

Jack's decision shows that he had learned an important lesson: You do what you have to do to survive. If you don't adapt to the reality of your surroundings, you will be destroyed. It's a lesson that is reflected again and again in Jack's later writings.

Jack was never content to stay in one place for very long. He wanted to see the places he had read about for himself. While he was still a very young man, he signed on as a sailor on a ship that traveled to Hawaii, Japan, and Alaska. An article of his, "Story of a Typhoon off the Coast of Japan," won first prize in a San Francisco newspaper competition. He rode the rails as a hobo (calling himself the "Frisco Kid") and traveled from California to

Chicago and then on to Michigan. At one point in his travels, he was charged with vagrancy—hanging around doing nothing—in Buffalo, New York. The local authorities threw him in jail for thirty days, a humiliating experience that left him with burning memories.

The jail time, and the ideas he was exposed to in his travels, motivated Jack to return to Oakland and finish high school. He even enrolled in college at one point, but he dropped out after a few months. As much as he loved reading and learning, he had trouble sitting still and being lectured to about the world around him—he wanted to be out there, experiencing it for himself. The funny thing, of course, is that his books would go on to be taught in many college-level literature classes—a notion that would have likely given Jack a good chuckle.

Along came the Gold Rush of 1897. Jack was 21 when he set off for the fabled gold-fields of Canada and, later, Alaska, as did many thousands of 'tenderfeet.' He found no gold, but he did find a very different sort of wealth: experiences that would later enable him to write great adventure stories of the frozen North. He returned from Alaska seriously ill with scurvy (a condition caused by lack of vitamin C) to find that his stepfather had died, leaving Jack's mother penniless. As he faced the responsibility of supporting his mother, Jack could see two paths open before him. One was to live his life as a "work beast," toiling like an animal in the factories where he had already spent too many brutal hours. The other was to seriously pursue a career as a writer. Jack took the second option.

Unlike many young people who dream of writing, Jack was extremely realistic in carrying out his plan. He had no romantic notions that inspiration would find him if he waited long enough. Instead, he set himself a strict schedule: he would write a minimum of 1,000 words every day. Within the next two years, although he collected hundreds of rejection slips, he published 24 pieces of writing, including short stories, jokes, poems, and essays. His first book, *The Son of the Wolf*, was published in 1900.

From that point on, Jack London's career soared. He published more than fifty books, including *White Fang* and *The Sea-Wolf*, hundreds of short stories, such as the immortal "To Build a Fire"; and countless articles on a wide range of topics. He reported on foreign wars, exposed horrible working conditions, and used his extensive travels on land and sea as material for his adventure novels.

People had never read anything quite like London's work. He was not only a distinctly American writer, but also a working-class writer with whom many readers could identify. Ordinary men and women appreciated London's sympathy for the underdog, for the working people who were all too often abused and exploited by people who were richer or better educated. At the same time, they were inspired by London's insistence that the individual must create his or her own future—as London himself had.

Even after London was wealthy enough to live comfortably wherever he chose, his thirst for adventure kept him on the move. With his wife, Charmian, he planned a seven-year sailing trip around the world, but ill health forced him home in less than a year. He traveled to Mexico to report on the revolution under way there, and wandered in Hawaii, Tahiti, Australia, Ecuador, Panama, and other faraway places. Health problems had always bothered him, but he had resisted settling long enough in one place to get consistent medical care. Finally, in 1916, his doctor warned him that his kidneys were failing. He returned to his ranch near Sonoma, California, and died there. He was only 40.

The final word on Jack London's brief, passionate life belongs to him. He wrote:

"I would rather be ashes than dust!
I would rather that my spark should burn out
in a brilliant blaze
than it should be stifled by dryrot.
I would rather be a superb meteor,
every atom of me in magnificent glow,
than a sleepy and permanent planet.
The proper function of man is to live,
not to exist.
I shall not waste my days in trying to
prolong them.
I shall use my time."

Jack London (1876 - 1916)

About *The Call of the Wild*

In 1903 Jack London wrote *The Call of the Wild*, a short novel about a dog. It became and remains a great classic of American literature, loved in many countries by five generations and translated into dozens of languages. The reason is simple: There are so many ways to enjoy the story.

At a basic level, it's exciting, easy to read, has non-stop action, and has a great protagonist, or main character. Authors spend long days and nights straining to produce characters like the dog Buck: noble, gutsy, and appealing. Like a great athlete running a marathon, London makes it look easy. Even if you're only interested in the surface meaning of the story, you can enjoy the adventure of *The Call of the Wild* for its own sake.

But for those who like to go deeper into the story, a little digging yields results. The story begins with Buck ripped away from a happy, safe environment and thrown into a vicious, merciless one. Many people, looking back, can see a parallel situation in their own lives, as they moved from happy, innocent childhood into the darker reality of growing up. Despite the odds, Buck has a spirit that won't quit: he adapts, survives, and lives while others do not. Adversity changes him, but it can't crush him, and in the end he triumphs. *The Call of the Wild* is a story about survival: about making your own way in a world that is not always kind.

In *The Call of the Wild*, London introduces many of his favorite themes. One of the most powerful is the idea that a kind of inner wisdom lives within all creatures—a wisdom that gets buried under layers of civilization. As Buck loses the rules and standards he has always lived by, we see him discovering that inner wisdom. The further he gets from the comfort of the judge's fireside, the more he must draw upon his instincts—things he just knows, handed down from his own distant wolf ancestry. There is a word for this process of reaching back to one's basic animal instincts: atavism. London uses the story to suggest that when the rules of civilization are taken away, we must revert to our own ancient instincts—that is, become atavistic. The story of Mercedes, Hal, and Charles illustrates what happens to creatures who fail to understand this law. We see them foolishly trying to bring their old, "civilized" way of life into the wilderness. Their pots and pans and canned goods weigh them down; their refusal to humble themselves and learn the ways of the wilderness eventually destroys them.

While Buck is shown relying on his long-buried instincts for his own survival, the story also speaks powerfully of the virtue of comradeship. Buck doesn't like all the other dogs equally—in fact, he hates Spitz—but that doesn't keep him from doing his job. He makes an excellent teammate, learning his duties quickly from the more experienced dogs. Even if he has negative feelings about a dog, he works with that dog to get the job done. At the book's end, when Buck becomes the leader of a truly wild pack of wolves, we see the wolves working together to hunt and survive. The wolves, too, know the value of comradeship.

If you're interested in doing your own writing, you can learn a lot from London's storytelling methods. His main character stands out from the rest. He develops a wide range of characters, and does so swiftly. He doesn't waste words; there is no 'filler.' He gets right to the point. Description is vivid and clear. He includes deep meaning, but crafts the story to be enjoyable for its own adventuresome sake. Suspense is constant. It's very hard to predict how the story will end.

We've only scratched the surface of all there is to discover in *The Call of the Wild*. You can easily find more with a close reading. Literary analysis is an important skill, and it is easier than it might seem at first. *The Call of the Wild* is an excellent book to work with, thanks to the clarity of London's writing and the many themes he weaves into a relatively short book.

The technique is simple: As you read the story, watch for themes and ideas that keep showing up. Ask yourself why those themes are important enough for the author to repeat.

It also helps to stop from time to time and think about what you feel as you read the story. Then, take what you notice in the book, and compare it to real life—maybe even to a similar experience you've had. Doing this will help you understand the deeper message of the book. Before you know it, you will be getting more out of the wonderful story of *The Call of the Wild* than you ever thought possible.

Enjoy your adventure!